A Girl From Flint

A Girl From Flint

Treasure Hernandez

www.urbanbooks.net

Urban Books, LLC
78 East Industry Court
Deer Park, NY 11729

A Girl From Flint Copyright © 2010 Treasure Hernandez

ISBN 13: 978-1-60162-473-4
ISBN 10: 1-60162-473-5

First Mass Market Printing November 2011
First Trade Paperback Printing February 2010
Printed in the United States of America

10 9 8 7 6 5 4 3 2 1

This is a work of fiction. Any references or similarities to actual events, real people, living, or dead, or to real locales are intended to give the novel a sense of reality. Any similarity in other names, characters, places, and incidents is entirely coincidental.

Distributed by Kensington Publishing Corp.
Submit Wholesale Orders to:
Kensington Publishing Corp.
C/O Penguin Group (USA) Inc.
Attention: Order Processing
405 Murray Hill Parkway
East Rutherford, NJ 07073-2316
Phone: 1-800-526-0275
Fax: 1-800-227-9604

Prologue

Karma is what put me in that hellhole. I don't even know how I ended up in jail. A couple of years ago, I was on top of the world. I've had more money flow through my hands than most people ever see in their entire lives. I was the woman that everybody wanted, and I had my way with some of the richest men in the Midwest. From prestigious businessmen to the most 'hood-rich niggas in Flint, I've had them all. We thought it was a game, and in a way, it was. We were trained to be the best. Skilled in the art of seduction, we were professionals who knew how to please in every sexual way. In my family, the mentality was if you ain't fucking, you don't eat.

Growing up in the 'hood, I had to use what I had to get what I wanted. My pussy was my meal ticket, and in order to stay on top, I juiced every nigga green to the game. I felt like if a dude was stupid enough to let me trick him out of his dough, then he deserved to get got. "Fuck me, pay me!" was our motto, and I used to laugh when my girls used to shout that after we hustled men out of their money.

It's not quite as funny these days though. Now I've got a prison sentence hanging over my head, and I'm locked in this cage like an animal. I haven't washed my hair in months, and I'm looking over my shoulder every minute of every day, hoping these bitches in here won't try to get at me. I don't know; maybe it was my destiny. With all the wrong that I've done, all that shit came back like a boomerang and hit me harder than I could have ever imagined. I sit in this jailcell every day, wondering how I landed in a state prison—a maximum-security state prison at that.

When I heard the judge say those words, it brought tears to my eyes. It was like a nightmare, and I was dreaming about my worst fear, only I couldn't wake up. It was real, and there was no waking up from it.

My downfall was . . . well, you'll learn about that later.

From the very beginning of my life, I was headed in a downward spiral. My mother is a crack fiend, and I haven't seen or spoken to her in years. I never knew my father. He died before I got the chance to get to know him. I hear that he really loved me, but the fact that he wasn't in my life affected me. I never had that male figure in my life, and that pains me greatly.

As you read this novel, understand that this is what happened to me, and that everything that you do has its consequences.

I remember we would talk about opening up our own salon and not needing a nigga to support us. That was before my life got complicated. Believe me, if I could turn back the hands of time, I would have never stepped foot in the murder capital, Flint, Michigan.

Yeah, that was the first of our mistakes. Honey made it seem so live, so wonderful. I thought it was the city that would make all my dreams come true. The truth of the matter is, everyone in that damn city has hidden agendas and is looking for a way to get paid, by any means necessary. I was a little girl trying to do big things in a small city. I should've just kept my ass in good ol' New York.

Me and my girls thought we were the shit. We got whatever we wanted, when we wanted it, from dick to pocketbooks, even first-class vacations around the world. We used men until their pockets ran out, and when we were done, we tossed them aside and moved along to the next one. Some people may call us hoes, gold-diggers, or even high-paid prostitutes, but nah, it wasn't like that. It was our hustle, and trust me, it paid well . . . very well.

I wish I could go back to the good ol' days when we used to smoke weed in Amra's room and open the windows so Ms. Pat wouldn't find out. Or the days when we used to lie about staying the night over each other's house so we could go to parties and stay out all night.

Those are the memories that make this place bearable. Those are the times that I reflect on when I get depressed and when life seems unfair. The times when it was just me, Honey, Amra, and Mimi, the original Manolo Mamis.

There have been many after us, but none like us. All them other bitches are just watered-down versions of what we used to be. That's who we were, that was our clique. That's the friendship that I miss, and think about when I feel lonely. The thought of how close we used to be is something I will cherish forever.

I know I'm rambling on and on about me and my girlfriends. You are probably wondering, *Bitch, how did you end up in jail?*

Damn, I'm so busy trying to tell y'all what happened, I forgot to introduce myself. I know y'all wanna read about Sunshine and Shai and all that high school bullshit, but let me get my piece off first. I promise you, you won't be disappointed. I'm Tasha, and this is my Flint story.

Chapter One

1994

As Lisa looked into the mirror, she could not recognize the eyes that stared back at her. Everything started running through her mind all at once. She thought about the loss of her only love, Ray, his death, and about their creation, Tasha. Tasha was the only positive thing in her life. Her bloodshot eyes stared into the mirror as she looked into her lifeless soul and began to cry.

Lisa tied a brown leather belt around her arm and began to slap her inner arm with two fingers, desperately searching for a vein. As the tears of guilt streamed down her face, she looked at the heroin-filled needle on the sink and reached for it. She hated that she had this terrible habit, but it called for her. She wasn't shooting up to get high anymore; she was doing it to feel better. She needed the drug. She tried to resist it, but the drug called out to her more and more. When she wasn't high, she was sick and in tremendous pain, and her body fiended for it.

She injected the dope into her vein, and a warm sensation traveled up her arm. The tears seemed to stop instantly, and her frail body slowly slumped to the floor, her eyes staring up into space. All of Lisa's emotions and her negative thoughts slowly escaped her mind as she began to smirk. She could not shake this habit that a former boyfriend had introduced her to, and her weekend binges eventually became an addiction.

Her addiction affected her life, as well as her daughter's. All of her welfare checks sponsored the local dope man's chrome rims, ice, and pocket money. Her life started going downhill after the death of Raymond Parks, better known as Ray.

It was 1982, the era of pimping. Lisa was fifteen when she met Ray, who was twenty-one at the time and a known pimp in the area. Ray approached Lisa while she was walking to the store. He pulled up and slyly said, "Hey, sweetness. Wanna ride?"

Lisa paid him no mind and kept walking. She started switching her ass a little harder while walking, knowing she had an audience. She pretended not to be flattered by the older man, and flipped her blond, sandy-brown hair.

Ray parked his long Cadillac at the corner and stepped his shiny gators onto the streets of Queens. He took his time, and eventually caught up with the thick young woman with hazel eyes. He slid in front of Lisa, blocking her path. "Hello, beautiful. My name is Raymond, but my friends call me Ray. I wouldn't have forgiven myself if I didn't take the time out to meet you." Ray stuck out his hand and offered a handshake.

Lisa looked up and saw a tall, lean, brown-skinned young man. She couldn't stop her lips from spreading, and she unleashed her pretty smile. She shook his hand and said with a shaky voice, "I'm Lisa."

Raymond smiled and stared into her eyes. Lisa stared back, and her eyes couldn't seem to leave his. He knew he had her when he saw that all too familiar look in her eyes. He asked in a smooth, calm voice, "Can I take you out sometime?"

"My mama might not like that."

Ray smiled. "Just let me handle her. So, can I take you out sometime or what?"

Lisa blushed. "Yeah, I guess that'll be all right."

Raymond gave her his number and asked her how old she was. Lisa told him that she was only fifteen. Ray's facial expression dropped, disappointed to know she was so young. He didn't usually approach girls her age, but she had an adult body, and was by far the most beautiful girl he'd ever seen. He grabbed her hand, looked at her, and told her to give him a call so he could pick her up later that day.

Lisa watched Ray get into his car and pull off. She couldn't stop smiling to herself as she continued to walk to the store. *He was a fly brother. I hope my momma lets me go.* She hurried to the store so she could get home and call Ray. She knew that it would take a miracle for her to get her mother's approval, but as fine as Ray was, she was definitely going to try.

Lisa called Ray later that evening, and an hour later he was at her front door with a dozen roses in each hand.

Lisa's mother answered the door and was impressed by the well-dressed young man that stood before her. She noticed he wasn't around Lisa's age and became skeptical about letting him in.

Ray sensed the vibe and quickly worked his magic. He handed the flowers to her and took off his hat to show respect. He didn't get to take Lisa out that night. He and Lisa's mother talked, and he charmed her for hours. He barely spoke to Lisa the entire evening. A professional at sweet-talking, he knew that to get Lisa, he had to get her mother first.

As the night came to an end, Ray said good-bye to Lisa's mother and asked if Lisa could walk him to his car. She agreed, and they exited the house.

Lisa and Ray stood in the driveway. He took her by the hand and said, "I never saw a lady so fly. I want you to be mine . . . eventually. What school do you go to?"

"McKinley."

Ray shook his head, then said in a soft voice, "I know where that's at. I'll pick you up after school tomorrow, okay?"

Lisa started to cheese. "Really?"

He grabbed Lisa's head, kissed her forehead softly, and whispered, "See you tomorrow."

She turned around and entered her mother's house, and Ray took off as soon as he saw that she got in safely.

The next day, Ray was parked outside of the high school in his Cadillac, waiting for his new "pretty young thang" as he called her. When she got into the car, Ray smiled at her. "Hello, beautiful. How was your day?"

From that day on, Ray and Lisa were together. He took her on shopping sprees weekly, and she was happy with her man. He never asked for sex and never rushed or pressured her in any way. Lisa wondered why the subject never came up, and wondered if he was physically attracted to her. Ray was very much attracted to her, but he'd promised himself he wouldn't touch her until she was eighteen. He had his hoes and women all over town, so sex was never an issue.

Lisa knew about his other women and his line of work, but never complained. Ray took care of her and treated her like a queen at all times. Over time, she fell deeply in love with him and never had a desire to mess with any other man.

Ray always made sure she had whatever she wanted, and that she went to school every day. If she didn't do well in school, her gifts would stop, so Lisa became a very good student.

Occasionally, Ray would help Lisa's mother with bills and put food in their refrigerator. Ray had money . . . real money. He was a pimp with hoes all over the city. He wasn't the type to put his hands on a woman. He made exceptions for the hoes that played with his chips or disrespected him. But in general, he had mind control over many women, so violence was rarely needed.

Exactly one month after her eighteenth birthday, Lisa found out she was pregnant with Ray's child. She couldn't believe she had gotten knocked up on her first time, but when she told him, he was the happiest man on earth. Lisa dropped out of school, and Ray immediately moved her from her mother's house and into his plush home in the suburbs.

He used to put his head on Lisa's stomach every night and tended to her every need. He promised that when he saved up enough money, he would open a business and exit the pimping game.

Eight months into her pregnancy, Lisa began to become jealous of Ray and all his women, and confronted him about it.

Ray reacted in a way that Lisa never saw. He raised his voice and said, "Don't worry about me and my business! You just have my baby, girl, and stand by yo' man!" He stormed out of the house and slammed the front door.

Lisa felt bad for confronting him and began to cry. She cried for hours, because she'd upset the only man she ever loved. Ray was all she knew. She stayed up and waited for his return, but he never came back.

That night, Ray went around town to collect his money from his workers. He was upset with himself for raising his voice at Lisa. He'd never yelled at her before, so it was really bothering him.

He pulled his Cadillac onto York Avenue and saw one of his best workers talking with a heavy-set man, about to turn a trick. He thought to himself, *Make that cheddar, Candy.* He decided to wait until Candy finished her business before collecting from her. He sat back in his seat, turned the ignition off, and listened to the smooth sounds of the Isley Brothers, and slowly rocked his head. He looked back at Candy, and noticed that she and the man were entering a car parked on the opposite side of the street. Candy was his "bottom bitch". She always kept cash flowing and never took days off. He smiled. *Candy's going to make that fool cum in thirty seconds.*

Suddenly, he saw Candy jump out of the car, spitting and screaming at the man. She walked toward the sidewalk spitting. The man jumped out of the car and started to yell at her, and yelled even louder when she kept on walking.

At this point, Ray calmly stepped out of the car and began to head toward her. The man had gotten to Candy and began to grab her and was screaming at the top of his lungs. Ray approached the man from behind and grabbed him. "Relax! Relax!"

"Mind yo' fucking business, playa! This bitch is trying to juke me out of my money!"

"Daddy Ray, he pissed in my mouth! He didn't say shit about pissing. I don't get down like that."

Before Ray could say anything, the man lunged at Candy, slamming her head hard into the brick wall she was leaning on. Ray immediately grabbed the man by the neck and began to choke him. His fingers wrapped tightly around his neck, Ray whispered to him, "Never put your hands on my hoes. If I see you around here again, it's you and me, youngblood." Ray released the man, and he dropped to the ground, trying to catch his breath. Ray stood over the man and pulled out a money clip full of cash. "How much did you give her?"

"Forty. I gave her forty," the man said, rubbing his neck.

Ray peeled off two twenties and threw it at the man and told him to get the fuck out of his office. The man took the money and ran to his car and pulled off.

Ray then turned around to help Candy up. She was lying motionless. He quickly bent down to aid her and noticed she wasn't breathing. He started to shake her and call her name, "Candy! Candy!" He got no response.

He gave her mouth-to-mouth resuscitation, and she began to breathe lightly. He knew he had to get her to the hospital, but he didn't want to be the one to take her in. It would raise suspicion if a known pimp brought a half-dressed hooker in, barely breathing and battered. He decided to search her purse to see if he could find a number for someone that she knew, so that they could check her into the hospital.

As soon as he stuck his hand in her purse, he saw flashing lights, and heard a man on a bullhorn telling him to put his hands up. Then another police car pulled up. Ray stood up, both of his hands in the air.

One of the police officers ran to the girl and put his fingers on her neck. He shook his head. The policemen handcuffed Ray and began to read him his rights.

"Wait, man, you got this all wrong—"

"Yeah, yeah." The cop led Ray to this police car.

Ray began to pull away from him. "Listen, I was helping her. I didn't—"

Another cop hit Ray over the head with a billyclub. "You got caught red-handed robbing this young lady. People like you make me sick."

Ray was too dazed to say anything as the cops put him in the back of the police car. He knew it looked bad for him. He dropped his head and began to pray.

The prosecutor stood up to give his closing argument. He wiped his forehead with a handkerchief, then slowly approached the jury. "The man sitting in that defendant's chair is a man of no remorse. He killed a seventeen-year-old girl in cold blood. Imagine if that girl was your daughter, your sister, or a beloved neighborhood child." He paused for effect. He wanted to give the jury time to process what he'd just said. He pointed his finger at Ray. "This man is a menace to society, and deserves to be punished to the fullest extent of the law. All of the evidence points toward one man. And that man is sitting before us today. That man is Raymond Parks. Nothing can keep our communities safe from this tyrant, except a life sentence. The only people who can make that happen are you, the people of the jury. Don't put another young girl in danger. Put him away for the rest of his life. He was caught over his victim's dead body, rummaging through her purse looking for money. He drove this woman's skull against a brick wall so hard and so violently, her brain hemorrhaged, which ultimately led to her death. How cold-blooded is that? So the prosecution asks of you—no, we beg of you, the jury, to sentence this man to a lifetime in prison. Render a guilty verdict and bring justice back to the community. I rest my case." The prosecuting attorney turned and walked back to his seat, a smug grin on his face. He knew he'd just delivered a closing argument that would cripple the defense and win the trial.

Ray looked back at Lisa and her swollen belly and felt an agonizing pain in his heart. He might spend the rest of his life in jail for a crime he didn't commit. He felt tears well up in his eyes as he mouthed the words, "I love you," to her.

Lisa looked into Ray's eyes and began to cry. She knew that the chances were slim for him to get off. She gripped the bench she was sitting on. *Please God, let them find him not guilty. Please! I need him,* she prayed as the jury deliberated in a private room.

Half an hour later, the jury returned to the courtroom with the verdict. An overweight old white man stood up and looked into Raymond's eyes and said, "We the jury, find the defendant, Raymond J. Parks, guilty of murder in the second degree, and guilty of strong-armed robbery."

Lisa screamed when the verdict was pronounced.

Ray dropped his head as the guards came over to escort him out of the courtroom. He looked at his attorney. "That's it? You said you could beat this case. I'm innocent, man. I'm innocent."

His attorney looked at him, shrugged his shoulders, and gave a sly smile. "We'll file an appeal."

Ray knew that his chances of winning the appeal would be just as slim as his chances of winning the trial. He looked at Lisa as they carried him out of the courtroom. "I love you," he mouthed again as the guards handcuffed him.

Lisa felt so much pain in her heart. She just stood there and watched her only love leave her life. Helpless, she didn't know what to do. Ray was going to prison, and there was nothing she could do to stop it from happening. She was so distraught, she couldn't control herself. She felt her dress become soaked and thought she had peed on herself. She felt liquid run down her legs, and then realized it wasn't urine. Her water had broken. "I'm going into labor!" she screamed to Ray just as the guards took him from her sight.

Her mother told her to sit down, and then called a guard over for help.

Later that evening, Tasha Parks was born. It was the worst day of Lisa's life. The love of her life had been convicted of murder, and ironically, their child was born on the same day.

Lisa was depressed for months and cried herself to sleep every night with her newborn baby in her arms.

Ray left behind a house and some money in the bank, so she supported herself and her daughter with that.

Lisa visited Ray as soon as they let her. He had grown a beard and walked to the table where a thick glass window separated them. She picked up the phone, and so did Ray. Ray did not have the same look in his eye that he used to have. The sparkle had diminished. Lisa desperately looked, trying to find a piece of the man she had fallen in love with, but it wasn't there. He had changed. There was no warm feeling in his eyes anymore, only coldness.

"How are you?" she asked, trying to be supportive.

Ray shook his head and smiled. "Don't worry about me. Just make sure you take care of our child. Lisa, I'm gon' be in here for a long time. I love you, and I want you to always remember that. I'll love you to the day I die."

Lisa noticed his hopeless vibe. It seemed as if he was telling her good-bye forever. "You're coming home, baby. Your lawyer is gon' file an appeal, and you're coming home."

Ray had to stop himself from becoming emotional. "That appeal is bullshit, baby. They are going to find me guilty, just like they did this time. That's even if the judge grants an appeal. Just remember I love you, and don't let my baby girl grow up not knowing that I love her too."

Lisa looked at their daughter, and then at Ray. "Tasha and I need you, Ray. You're all we got. We need you." She put her hand on the glass.

A single tear streamed down Ray's face. "*Tasha*? That's my baby girl's name? Make sure you tell her I love her. Every day, make sure that she knows that." He rose from his seat, kissed his fingers, and pressed them against the glass. He then began to walk out.

Lisa gripped the phone tightly and banged it against the glass, "No!" she screamed. "Ray, I love you! I love you!"

Ray walked back over to the glass and picked up the phone. "I love you, Lisa, but don't come here again. I don't want you or my daughter to see me in here. You deserve more. I love you." With those words, he headed to the cage that would be his home for the rest of his life.

A few weeks later, Lisa was breast-feeding Tasha when she received a phone call. She felt the floor spinning as she tried to understand the news from the other end. When she was sure she'd heard what the voice said, she dropped the phone and fell to her knees, her baby in the other arm. "No!" she screamed as she cried. Tasha was startled by her mother's roar and began to cry too.

A fellow inmate had stabbed Ray to death fifteen times in the chest.

Lisa sank into a deep depression and moved back home with her mother after Ray's death. She would go for weeks at a time without talking to anyone or even bathing. She often blamed herself for Ray's death, believing he wouldn't have stormed out of the house if she hadn't confronted him that night. *He would have stayed home with me,* she often thought to herself.

Lisa, looking for the same love that Ray had shown her, began to let men manipulate her into doing what they pleased. Any man who dressed nice and approached her had a chance. It became a problem when her mother grew tired of caring for Tasha while Lisa ran the streets.

Four years after Ray's death, another death was about to hit Lisa, her mother's. When Lisa's mother died, she finally felt the burden of being a mother. Tasha had grown so attached to her grandmother that she thought she was her mother, and called her Mama. She called Lisa by her first name.

Lisa met a man by the name of Glenn, a pimp in the neighborhood. He was in no way as successful as Ray, but Lisa was drawn to him. In some way, he reminded her of Ray.

Glenn introduced Lisa to weed. She liked the way it made her feel and began to smoke it so much, it didn't get her high anymore. Then, he introduced her to cocaine, telling her, "It makes you feel good."

Lisa used to snort a little cocaine with Glenn, but that quickly grew old. Eventually, she needed a new high, and Glenn provided that too. And so it was then that she got hooked on heroin.

Chapter Two

I forgot how much I hate school, Tasha thought as she heard the irritating shrill of her alarm. She drowsily reached over and hit the snooze button. She looked at her clock and got out of the bed. *Seven o'clock is too early to be getting out of bed,* she thought to herself on her way to the bathroom.

She opened the bathroom door and saw her mother leaning over the toilet, a scene she'd witnessed many times. Tasha's eyes filled with tears as she closed the bathroom door and walked down the hallway to return to her room. She had witnessed her mother use heroin before, but every time it happened, it hurt her even more than the time before. Her life didn't seem fair. She was only sixteen, but had seen things . . . so many things over the years, it had almost hardened her. Her mother's addiction was never a secret to her. Tasha knew what heroin was before she knew how to spell, and her rough childhood was something that she resented her mother for.

Everybody else seemed to have it easy, at least easier than she did. While her friends were complaining about how much they wished their parents would leave them alone, Tasha yearned to know what it was like to have someone who cared about her, a real mother who yelled and nagged.

She hated her mother more than anyone in the world. She was embarrassed by her. Lisa would do anything to feed her habit, and Tasha wasn't dumb to this fact. She knew that all the men that ran in and out of their house were there for only two reasons—to give her mother drugs, and to receive payment for those drugs. And since Lisa didn't even have money to keep clothes on her daughter's back or food in their refrigerator, Tasha knew how Lisa was paying the drug dealers. Lisa had become the neighborhood ho, spreading her legs for any man who could give her a temporary fix.

Tasha looked in the mirror and admired her brown skin and hazel eyes. She looked at a picture of her mother that sat on her dresser. It was taken before her mother had become addicted to drugs. She put the picture face down on her dresser and picked out some clothes to wear to school.

Tasha didn't have a lot of clothes, so her best friend, Amra had let her borrow an outfit to wear on the first day. She got ready for school and walked out of the house without even saying good-bye to her mother. She walked the five blocks to Amra's house, hoping she would be ready to go. She didn't want to be late on the first day.

Tasha knocked on Amra's door, and Ms. Pat answered and greeted Lisa with a familiar smile. "Hey, Tasha, baby. How are you?" She opened the door and motioned for her to come in. "Amra is upstairs getting dressed, but I made you two breakfast. You know, I want y'all to have a fresh start for the new school year."

Tasha smiled. She loved Ms. Pat as if she was her own mother. Ever since she could remember, Ms. Pat had been there for her.

Ms. Pat knew about Tasha's mother and thought Tasha was too good of a girl to have to go through that, so her door was always open to Tasha. "Why don't you go tell Amra to hurry her slow butt up before this food gets cold?"

Tasha laughed at Ms. Pat and ran up the stairs and into her friend's room.

Amra looked into her mirror and saw Tasha enter the room. "Hey, girl. Do these look right?" She turned around to look at her ass in the mirror. She was wearing skintight Baby Phat jeans and a matching wife-beater.

Tasha shrugged her shoulders. "Yeah, you look good, so get out the mirror and let's go."

Amra put on her gold hoop earrings and went extra slow just to irritate Tasha. "I'm so tired of school. One more year of this bullshit, and then I'm grown." She grabbed her bookbag off her bed.

They walked downstairs then into the kitchen and sat at the table. They ate breakfast together, then headed out the door for school.

"What classes you got?" Tasha asked.

Amra reached into her bookbag, pulled out her schedule, and handed it to Tasha for her to compare.

"Damn, we don't even have any classes together." Tasha handed both schedules to Amra.

"That's because you taking some hard-ass classes. You know I go for the easy A's," Amra said, half-joking.

Tasha was only in the eleventh grade, but she was taking twelfth grade English and science. Those were her best subjects, so it really didn't intimidate her. Because of her dysfunctional home life, she threw herself into school and worked extremely hard to make sure her grades were on point. "Whatever! Just meet me after school."

They parted ways, and Tasha walked to her English class. She walked in and took a seat near the back of the class.

Soon after, the teacher walked in and said, "Hi. I'm Mr. Benton, and I would like to welcome you all to my class. Now, one of you is joining this class as a junior," he said as he looked for his attendance sheet. "Tasha Parks?"

Tasha raised her hand. "Yeah, that's me."

"It's nice to meet you, Tasha," Mr. Benton stated. "Now, since you're a junior, I'm sure you will have some questions regarding some of the writing techniques used in this course, so I want you to feel comfortable asking anything you like,"

Tasha smiled back. *Damn! He ain't have to put me on blast like that!* "Okay."

After school, Tasha and Amra met up and began to walk home. "Did you see ol' boy today?" Tasha asked Amra.

Just as Amra was about to respond, a group of girls came up to them. "Ain't you the little bitch that tried to talk to Dre today?" one of them asked.

Amra stopped walking and looked at the girl. "Yeah. Who is you?" Amra wasn't a fighter, but she had the mouth of one.

"Bitch, I'm his girlfriend, and you need to stay your young ass out his face."

The girl was getting closer and closer to Amra's face, and Tasha didn't want her friend to have to fight. She said, "Look, she didn't know that Dre even had a girlfriend, so you need to be checking him about that, not her." She tried to sound as nice as she possibly could, not wanting to start beef with anybody, especially not with a senior.

Amra, surprised that Tasha had said anything, looked at her. *Ahh shit! We both about to get our asses beat!* She looked at the crowd of girls gathered around them and clenched her fists. *Shit, if I'm gonna fight, I might as well just hit her first.*

A girl walked through the crowd and stepped in the middle of the confrontation. "Sade, chill with this shit," she said.

Sade replied, "Honey, this ain't got nothing to do with you, so why you so concerned?"

Honey looked at Amra and Tasha. " 'Cuz them my little sisters, and yo' ass wouldn't say shit to nobody else for talking to Dre, so don't be trying to check them about it. Yo' scary ass trying to front because they juniors. You wouldn't be talking shit to me or any other senior girl if they were with Dre."

Sade rolled her eyes with an attitude and said, "Whatever!" then walked away.

Tasha's heart slowly stopped racing, and Amra sighed in relief.

"Damn, Tasha! Where all them balls come from? I thought you would have let me get my ass beat," Amra joked.

Tasha shrugged her shoulders. "You know it ain't even like that."

After the crowd dispersed, Honey approached the two girls. "Don't worry about Sade. That bitch be fronting. She wouldn't bust a grape in a fruit fight."

They started laughing.

Honey introduced herself, "I'm Honey."

Tasha and Amra introduced themselves, and then Honey walked away.

"Honey looked out because I wasn't trying to fight over a nigga," Amra stated as they started their walk home.

"Yeah. It seems like she cool people."

They arrived at Amra's house first, and then Tasha continued the walk to her house. "Call me later!" Tasha yelled. She dreaded going home to her mother, Lisa.

She slowly walked down the streets, hoping that her mother would be gone when she got there.

When Tasha walked into the house, like always, there was a new man lying up with her mother. Tasha smelled liquor. In fact, the house reeked of it, and she could tell that her mother was high. She had this dumb look on her face every time she got high, a look Tasha had come to know.

She rushed to her room and locked her bedroom door. *I am so tired of living here. I can't wait until I'm eighteen. I swear to God, I hate her!*

Tasha watched TV and did her homework for a couple hours. Her mother accumulated more and more company, and when they became too loud for Tasha to concentrate, she turned on her radio and fell asleep.

The next morning, Tasha awoke and got ready for school. She went downstairs and found her mother passed out on the couch in the living room. She shook her head in disgust and walked out of the front door before her mother had the chance to wake up and chastise her.

That morning at school, she noticed that Honey was in her English class. She didn't say anything to her though, she just went to her seat.

At lunch, Honey saved two seats for Tasha and Amra at the senior table. "Hey, come chill with us," she said as they started to walk past the table.

They sat down and immediately clicked. Honey was real cool, and she was always talking about dudes and money. "Y'all should come with me to this party. It's at Wayne State tonight, and it's supposed to be jumping."

Amra looked at Honey. "All right. I'll just have to make up something to tell my moms, because she is not about to let me go to no damn college party."

Honey laughed. "The party doesn't start until nine o'clock, so I'll just come over after school and say that I'm tutoring you. And then I'll ask if you can spend the night at my spot."

Amra didn't know if her mother would buy that, but she agreed anyway.

"What about you, Tasha?"

Tasha looked up. "Oh, I'm down. My momma won't care. I'm going over Amra's today anyway, so I'll already be out." She didn't know Honey very well, and didn't want everybody to know how her home life was, so she just left it at that.

Honey smiled. "All right then. Meet me in front after school, and we will ride to your house together."

Tasha was excited about going to a college party and couldn't concentrate on any of her classes. She just wanted the day to be over with fast. As soon as the bell rang, she walked outside and waited on Amra and Honey. They came out of the school together, and they all walked to Honey's car and got into a Nissan Maxima.

Amra asked, "Is this your whip?"

Honey shook her head. "Nah, this is my momma's car."

Honey stopped at her house first. She went in and came out a couple minutes later.

When they pulled up to Amra's house, they got out and went in. "Mama!" Amra shouted as soon as she walked in.

Ms. Pat walked down the stairs. "I'm right here, Amra. You don't got to be screaming at the top of your lungs." She walked over to her daughter and gave her a kiss, then gave Tasha a kiss. "How was school?" she asked.

The girls shrugged their shoulders, and then Amra replied, "It was good. Hey, Ma, this is our friend, Honey. She's a senior. She came over to help us with our math."

Ms. Pat smiled warmly at Honey. "It's nice to meet you, sweetie. It's about time these girls got another friend. Are you girls hungry?"

They shook their heads no, and headed up to Amra's room. Amra turned on her radio, and Honey and Tasha flopped down on the bed.

"So what are y'all wearing tonight?" Honey asked.

Amra went to her closet. "I don't know. What are you wearing?"

Honey grabbed her bookbag and pulled out a pink and white Baby Phat outfit. Honey pulled out two more outfits, another Baby Phat and a Rocawear. "Y'all can wear one of these if you want to." She got in the mirror and started fixing her hair.

Tasha watched Honey swoop her hair up into a ponytail. "You know how to do hair?" she asked.

"Yeah. I'll hook you up if you need me to."

The girls primped and groomed until they were ready to go to the party. Honey had her hair swooped into a ponytail, Amra had her hair flat-ironed down, and Tasha had cornrows to the back, with big hoop earrings.

Honey put the outfits back in her bookbag. "Y'all can get dressed in the car."

Amra looked at Tasha and Honey. "Okay. Where I am I going tell my momma we going?"

Honey stood up. "I'll tell her something."

They grabbed the bookbag full of clothes and walked downstairs, where Ms. Pat was sitting in the living room, reading a magazine.

"Hey, Ma, can we go out with Honey?"

Ms. Pat looked up. "You girls look nice. But where are you trying to go?"

"Well, we just want to go and see a movie. It starts at ten, and my mother let me get her car tonight so we could go and see it." The words rolled off Honey's tongue like a professional as she fed Ms. Pat the lie.

"Do you have a driver's license?"

Honey took her license out of her bookbag and showed it to Ms. Pat.

"I guess it's okay then, but y'all better be back here by one o'clock."

The girls jetted out the door. As they drove downtown, Honey said, "It's these dudes that are going to be at this party. They got money. I have been kicking it with one of them on MySpace."

Tasha frowned. "MySpace?"

"He was the one who bought me those outfits y'all got on. His boys got just as much money as he do, so y'all better get on 'em."

Tasha quickly learned that Honey knew how to talk a nigga out of money. They never bought her anything big, but she always kept new shoes, tight clothes, and extra cash. Every weekend, the girls would chill, and every time they got together, Honey had something new to show them.

Tasha and Amra quickly adapted to Honey's ways. They had plenty of boys at their high school falling in love with them. Amra had even snatched Dre up from under Sade. It was crazy.

Anything they wanted, they quickly got just by letting a nigga think he was special.

As Honey, Tasha, and Amra grew closer and closer, together they hit more niggas for more things.

"Tony's stupid ass gave me a hundred dollars today." Amra pulled it out of the Coach purse another boy had purchased for her about a month ago. "His ugly ass will give me anything I want."

Tasha laughed. "Niggas is stupid. All you got to do is tell 'em you love 'em, and they be willing to give you anything you want."

Honey shook her head. "It ain't the love they want, it's that ass. You know niggas be trying to fuck, and they will pay any amount for some pussy. You just got to get that shit out of 'em. I let them dudes know up front that I ain't fucking for free."

Tasha responded, "Shit, ain't no nigga fucking me for no cash. I ain't even on that level yet. I just be playing with their heads a little bit."

Amra walked over to her dresser and put the money in her panty drawer. "That's why we be getting more money than you. Please believe, them niggas will pay for it. Tasha, you better be real and get them for they money." Amra reached for the blunt that Honey had just rolled up, something she had picked up from Honey.

She hit it and slowly inhaled and passed the weed to Tasha.

She shook her head. "No, I'm straight."

Honey took the blunt from Amra and laughed.

"What you scared of?" Amra opened up her bedroom window, so her mother wouldn't smell the weed.

"Nothing. I just don't smoke."

They chilled for a couple hours, then Honey drove Tasha home. They pulled up to Tasha's house, said their good-byes, and Tasha got out of the car.

When Tasha walked into her house, Lisa, high as usual, approached her, so Tasha just kept walking toward her room.

"Where the fuck you been, you little bitch? I told you to come home after school. I needed you to do something."

Tasha just ignored her mother. She wasn't even making sense. She hadn't even talked to her mother for a couple of days, since Ms. Pat had been letting her stay the night at her house. She saw a strange man sitting on the couch and knew that her mother had company.

Lisa pulled Tasha's arm as she tried to walk past her. "Don't you walk your fast ass away from me. Momma needs a favor."

Tasha snatched her arm from her mother's grasp.

Lisa smacked her across the face. "I told you about disrespecting me. I'm still your momma."

I'm tired of this shit. I'm so tired of this. I'm out. Tasha walked into her room to get the money she'd been saving up. She looked in the shoebox under her bed, but it was empty.

Her mother came and stood in her door. "Oh, I took that. You should've brought your ass home. How you get that money? Yo' little ho ass out here tricking?"

Tears came to Tasha's eyes. She grabbed a bag and went to her closet and started throwing her clothes into it. She grabbed the picture of her once normal mother and put that in the bag as well. *I don't have to deal with this,* she thought, tears streaming down her face. She grabbed her bag and ran out of her room. She walked into the living room and attempted to walk out the door, but her mother's friend was blocking it. "Move the fuck out my way!" Tasha yelled. "I don't know you!" She attempted to shove him out of her way.

The strange man grabbed her and held her close to him . . . too close to him. Tasha started twisting and kicking to get out of his grasp. "Let me go! What the fuck are you doing?" she screamed. She felt a hard bulge in his pants. "Get the fuck off me!"

"He just wants to give you a little kiss, Tasha. Sit yo' fast ass down. Do Momma this favor," Lisa said as she watched her friend run his hands all over her daughter's body. She walked over to Tasha and said, "Relax, baby. It won't take long. He got a big juicy dick. He gon' make you feel good."

Tasha kicked and screamed as the man and her mother tried to lay her down on the floor. In a panic, she started to scream as loud as she could.

The man put his hand over her mouth to shut her up, unbuttoning her pants with the other hand. Tasha kicked to try and ward him off. She bit hard into his flesh.

He raised his hand back and smacked her hard in the face, and Tasha felt the tingles vibrate in her face. He raised his hand again and hit her hard across the face a second time.

Tasha screamed out in pain, "Stop it! Help me! Momma, stop!" She screamed as she felt her mother hold her legs down.

All of the sudden, Tasha heard a thud and saw the man grab the back of his head and crawl off, swearing to himself.

"Get the fuck off of her!" Honey said as she helped Tasha up.

Tasha watched the man holding the back of his head and heard her mother yelling at Honey.

Honey pushed Lisa out of the way, grabbed Tasha's bag off of the floor, and dragged Tasha out of the house. "Are you okay?" she asked, hugging her.

"I just need to get out of here." Tasha huffed through her tears. "Can you take me to Amra's?"

The car was silent on the way there. Honey couldn't believe what she had just witnessed. The only reason why she'd come back was because Tasha had left her purse in her car. *No wonder she never liked to talk about her momma.* Honey patted Tasha's hand to reassure her that everything would be all right. *If I hadn't shown up when I did, who knows what they would have done to her. That's fucked-up, her own mother would try to rape her.*

They arrived at Amra's house and rang the doorbell a thousand times before Amra answered it.

Amra opened the door and saw Tasha in tears. She knew something serious had happened. "Ma!" Amra yelled, knowing that her mother would know what to do.

Ms. Pat came rushing downstairs and saw that Tasha was hysterical, and that the side of her face was red and swollen. "Oh, baby, come here," she cooed softly. She embraced Tasha, and tears formed in her own eyes. "You're not going back to that house. You are okay now. It's going to be all right." Ms. Pat hugged Tasha and rocked her back and forth as if she were a baby.

Honey called her own mother and told her what had happened, and let her know that she would be spending the night at Amra's.

Ms. Pat finally calmed Tasha down and tucked her into Amra's bed. Amra and Honey slept on the floor and tried to comfort their friend. Ms. Pat brought Tasha some ice for her face and said, "Try and get some sleep, Tasha. You are safe now. I'm not letting you go back to that damn house."

Tasha had finally stopped crying. "Why would she do this to me?" she asked. Her voice was raw and her face flush.

"Your mother has a lot of demons that she's dealing with, baby. She can't take care of you right now. There are other people in your life that love you, Tasha. Look at these fools right here." Ms. Pat pointed to Honey and Amra. "They love you more than anyone in the world, and you are like a daughter to me."

All three girls laughed.

"Thank you, Ms. Pat," Tasha whispered.

Patricia turned off the room light and closed the bedroom door.

The girls lay there in awkward silence, not knowing what to say. Tasha was embarrassed, hurt, and confused. Honey and Amra were both shocked. Neither girl knew what to say to make her feel better.

I couldn't imagine going through something like that, Amra thought to herself.

"How could she do this? I'm her daughter." Tasha said through tears of pain.

Honey sat up. "Fuck her, Tasha! We love you."

"We are your family, and we ain't gon' let nothing else happen to you."

Honey couldn't imagine how Tasha was feeling, but she knew Amra was right. She couldn't let anything else happen to Tasha. She was like the sister that Honey never had.

Honey turned to Amra and Tasha and said, "To none of us! Fuck that! We are too close. Ain't nothing gonna happen to you, Tasha, or you, Amra. Y'all my girls for real, and we got to look out for each other. We can't let anybody else hurt us. We always got to stick together. We don't trust anybody but each other."

Tasha nodded her head and hugged her two best friends. They were the only people in this world she could trust and depend on.

Tasha left home and moved in with Amra and Ms. Pat, and the bond between the girls only grew stronger throughout the rest of the school year. They were inseparable; whenever you saw one, you saw the other two.

They continued to hit niggas for money, but as the school year came to an end and Honey was getting ready to graduate, the clique grew restless.

"Why you got to go all the way out there?" Tasha asked Honey as they were lying on Amra's floor, watching a movie.

"Me and my cousin, Mimi, are supposed to be trying to open up a hair salon. Y'all know I love to do hair and shit."

Amra smacked her lips. "I'm saying though, you my girl, and Michigan is so far away."

"Y'all need to be trying to come with me. I know that my auntie would let y'all stay with her, at least temporarily. We could get our own apartment. Just say, 'Fuck it, fuck school,' and come with me."

Tasha wasn't feeling that idea. She wasn't trying to jump stupid and become a high school dropout. "Fuck that! I ain't dropping out of school. That's some dumb shit. I mean, we hustling niggas and everything, but that shit ain't gon' pay no bills. It ain't gon' bring no security.

I can't fuck with y'all on that." Tasha's education was important to her, and was the only thing that gave her hope.

"Yeah, Honey, she's right. My momma would look at me like I'm crazy if I asked her if I could move out there with you."

"I mean, don't trip though, y'all. We still got the whole summer to spend together. Then after we graduate high school next year, we can come out to Flint and hustle those niggas right."

Tasha wasn't trying to think about the day that their threesome would become a twosome. They were all together now, and that's all that mattered.

The girls changed the subject. None of them wanted to think about the end of the summer when Honey would leave her friends.

Chapter Three

Tasha and Amra watched Honey walk across the stage in June. They were the loudest people at the graduation ceremony. They just couldn't help themselves, they were proud of their friend.

"That bitch done graduated and shit!" Amra clapped loudly for Honey as she accepted her diploma.

They sat through the rest of the commencement in silence, and after it was over, they ran over to Honey and gave her a hug.

"Congratulations!" Tasha sang. She hugged her friend tight.

"Thanks, girl. Come on, I want y'all to meet my momma." Honey pulled them over to a woman that could have been her twin. She had the same dark chocolate skin, long hair, and thin frame that her daughter displayed so well. They were truly model-type women. "Ma, this is Tasha and Amra."

"Hi, girls. You can call me Ms. Jones. I have heard so much about the two of you. It's nice to finally meet you."

"Ma, can we use the car today?"

Ms. Jones smiled. "Yes, just drop me off at home and then have fun tonight. You don't have to worry about being home at a certain time. It's your big day. Enjoy it."

Honey, Tasha, and Amra got into the Nissan, and they dropped Honey's mother off at home.

"Have fun, and don't bring my car back with no dents in it." Ms. Jones got out of the car and went into the house.

"So, where y'all trying to go?"

Tasha shrugged her shoulders. "I don't know. What's popping tonight?"

Honey looked in her rearview at Amra. "Well, the club is gon' be jumping tonight. A lot of graduations were today, so you know all the graduates gon' be trying to be up in there."

Amra sat up and stuck her head in between the front seats. "You know me and Tasha ain't gon' be able to get into the damn club."

"Yeah, you will. They don't even be carding like that. I heard that they rarely even check ID's. So are we out?"

Tasha put in a CD and turned up the volume. "We out, and if we don't get in, then we'll just do something else. I'm hungry right now anyway, so let's go eat."

The girls went to Applebee's and celebrated Honey's graduation.

"Here are the invitations to my open house. My senior pictures are in there too." Honey pulled two envelopes from her purse and put them on the table. They picked them up.

Amra said, "You know we gon' be there."

"Your pictures are cute."

Honey fanned herself and jokingly said, "I know."

The girls laughed, and then ate their food.

Tasha looked at her two friends, and was filled with sadness as she realized that this summer would be the last summer that they had to chill with Honey. It would be a long time before they saw her again. *Her ass moving all the way to the Midwest and shit,* she thought as she ate her food. Tasha knew Honey needed to go to Flint, but that didn't make it any easier for her to let go of one of her best friends.

"You ready to go?" Amra asked Tasha for the second time.

Tasha came out of her thoughts and got up and walked out of the restaurant with Amra and Honey behind her.

That night outside the club, the line was extra long. It seemed like everybody was trying to get up in there. A group of girls walked back from the front of the line. One of them muttered on their way back to the parking lot, "Fuck this! Them lame-ass bouncers could have let us in."

Amra overheard the comment. She turned to Tasha. "See, I told y'all they was gon' be checking ID's."

"Girl, chill the fuck out. They gon' definitely spot your underage ass if you go up there tripping."

Honey laughed. "Hell, yeah. Just chill and we in there."

The girls waited in the line for about twenty minutes before they grew restless. Amra thought as she stood in the line, *My damn feet hurt. If I would have known we was gon' be waiting like this, I would have worn some kicks.*

As if Tasha had read Amra's mind, she turned to Honey. "Fuck this! Let's go somewhere else. My feet are starting to hurt."

Honey nodded her head in agreement, and they started to turn and go back to the car. Just as they were getting ready to get into Ms. Jones's car, a pearl white Cadillac Escalade pulled up next to them. The driver rolled down the window and said, "What up, ma?"

Tasha turned around and looked at the driver. *Damn! He fresh to death!* she thought as she approached his window.

Honey and Amra waited by the car, as Tasha went over to talk to the carful of dudes.

"What up, li'l mama? Where y'all going?" the dude asked her, trying to sound cool.

Tasha glanced back at her girls. "I don't know, but it's too packed up in there. We ain't trying to be in line all night."

The dude licked his lips. "What's your name?"

"Tasha."

The dude stuck his hand out of the window and shook Tasha's hand. "I'm Damon."

"It's nice to meet you, Damon, but we're about to go."

Damon looked at his boys in the back of the car. "You and your girls over there can come into the party with us if you want to. I'ma go park. Just meet us at the front."

Tasha told Damon to hold on and then went back over to her friends. "Hey, he can get us in."

Honey and Amra locked their doors.

"His friends better not be ugly!" Amra commented.

Honey laughed, and they walked over to the group of guys.

Damon put his arm around Tasha, and they walked to the front of the line and into the club. As soon as she walked in, it felt like everybody in the club was staring at her. She could feel the jealousy in the room as all the females wondered who she was. Tasha didn't care, though.

The music in the club was loud, and everybody seemed to be having a good time. She followed Damon to the VIP section. Honey and Amra sat across from her with two of Damon's friends. Damon whispered into her ear, "You want a drink or something?"

Tasha had never had a sip of liquor before in her life, and didn't think it was appropriate for her to experiment with a nigga she barely knew. "No, I'm good."

The evening was fun, and they celebrated Honey's graduation until 2:00 A.M.

When they walked out of the club, Damon was feeling Tasha. He walked her over to Honey's car. "So, you got a number where I can reach you?"

Tasha knew that Damon was older than she was. He had to be at least twenty-one, and she didn't want someone that old calling her at Ms. Pat's house. "No, but you can give me yours."

Damon laughed. "All right. I can feel that."

Tasha took out a piece of paper, and Damon wrote his telephone number on it. "I guess I'll holla at you later then," she said in a flirtatious way. She walked back to her friends while Damon watched her get in the car.

"Damn, Tasha! That nigga was all on your ass tonight."

Honey had noticed it too. "Yeah, girl. You better get on his ass. He got bread. Did you see the car he was driving?"

Tasha laughed at her two friends, always talking about money. "Yeah, I guess he was cool. He old as hell, though."

Honey frowned up her face. "Girl, please. That nigga's only twenty. That's only four years older than you. And he got bank. And you had all them bitches in the club jealous of you. Money don't got no age. You better get at that mu'fucka." Honey smiled to herself, thinking about how much money she would get out of Damon if she had him. "You know that nigga fly, and if you don't want him, I'll take him."

"I don't know. I might call him," Tasha said with a smile. She had to admit, Damon was fine as hell, and from the looks of him, he was caked up.

Honey laughed, looked at Amra, then they both said, "She gon' call him."

Honey pulled up in front of Amra's house at two thirty in the morning. Amra looked up at the dark house. "I hope my momma's sleep."

Honey laughed. "Just go in quietly."

Tasha and Amra got out of the car and approached the house. Tasha was nervous as hell. Even though Ms. Pat wasn't her mother, Ms. Pat would still get in her ass.

Amra put her key in the door and opened it quietly, trying to stop it from creaking. When she saw that the house was still on the inside, she motioned for Tasha to come in, and they both crept up the stairs and into the room that they shared. When they finally got in, they both burst out laughing.

"You won't be laughing when your momma come in here," Tasha said, teasing her friend.

"Bitch, neither will you."

The next day, Tasha was home alone. The school year was over, Amra had to go to summer school, and Ms. Pat worked from eight until three. She picked up the phone and called Honey, "Hey, B. What you doing?" she said when Honey finally picked up the phone.

"Girl, trying to sit down and help my momma plan this open house. What are you doing?"

"Nothing. Just sitting over here bored. I'm not gonna hold you up, but call me when you get done." Tasha hung up the phone and grabbed her purse off the nightstand. *I guess I can call him,* she thought to herself.

Tasha began to dial Damon's number. She regretted it almost as soon as she punched in the last digit. The phone started to ring. *Damn! I shouldn't have called him yet.* She was relieved when his voice mail picked up. She hung up without leaving a message.

As soon as she was about to go downstairs, the phone rang. "Hello?" She expected to hear Honey's voice.

"Hello. Did somebody just call my phone?"

Tasha knew it was Damon. She didn't know what to say though. She didn't want him to think that she was whack or desperate to get at him. "Yeah, this is Tasha."

"What up?"

There was a long silence, and Tasha felt stupid for calling him.

"Look I'm a little busy right now, but can I holla at you later? Come see you or something?"

Tasha didn't want Damon to call back to the house when Ms. Pat was home. "Yeah, you can come pick me up."

"All right, give me about an hour."

Tasha gave him directions to the house. She was smiling from ear to ear. *I cannot believe I*

*just told him that he could come over. I don't
even know him like that.*

Tasha figured it was too late for her to back
out, so she got dressed. She put on a tight-fitting
black skirt with a black halter top that showed
her flat stomach.

She flat-ironed her hair, and an hour later, she
was waiting for Damon to come.

Damon pulled up to her house at two o'clock,
and she walked out to his truck. "What up?" She
opened the door to enter his truck.

He looked at her, nodded his head. "You hungry?"

Tasha was hungry, but she didn't want to eat
in front of him. *Damn, I'm trying to get my grub
on. Ain't nobody trying to eat cute.* She said yes
anyway, though, and he took her to Red Lobster,
where she ordered a salad. When their food arrived, Damon's plate made Tasha's stomach
growl. She looked down at her salad, and then
looked across the table at his plate and thought,
Damn! But, of course, she ate like a lady and
didn't even finish the whole salad.

After leaving the restaurant, they went to a
movie. Tasha had to admit that even though she
had her doubts about Damon, she felt comfortable around him. *And he is paying for everything,* she thought as she ordered a frozen slush
from the snack stand at the movies.

When it was time for her to go home, she knew Ms. Pat would be home because it was seven o'clock. She had Damon drop her off at Honey's house.

"So, when I'm gon' see you again?" he asked as he pulled up in front of Honey's house.

Tasha smiled. "I don't know, 'cuz I don't really have a number that you can call me on."

Damon handed her his cell phone. "Holla at me."

"How I'm gon' call you if I got your phone?"

Damon licked his lips. "I got another one. The number's programmed in the phone already, so holla at me."

Tasha smirked at him. *This nigga think he cute.* She took the phone and got out of the car, and he waited to make sure that she got in the house.

Honey opened the door and saw Damon pulling away from her house. "No, you didn't! You called him? No, you didn't! What y'all do?" she asked as Tasha walked into her house.

Tasha tried to act calm, but Honey could see the smile on her face. "Ask your momma if you can take me home," Tasha said.

Honey took Tasha to Ms. Pat's house. When Tasha got out, Honey yelled, "I'm gon' call you when I get home, and you better tell me everything."

Tasha laughed. She held up Damon's cell phone. "I'll call *you!*"

Honey screamed, "Aww, bitch! No, you didn't! He bought you a phone? Damn! You just met his ass last night."

Even though Damon didn't actually buy Tasha the phone, she let her girl think that. *She ain't got to know everything.* "Look, though, I'll call you later."

Honey sped off, and Tasha went into the house. Tasha saw Ms. Pat sitting in the kitchen. "Hi, Ms. Pat. How was work?"

Ms. Pat looked up from the paper she was reading. "It was fine. What did you spend the day doing?"

"Nothing. Went over to Honey's house and was chilling with her all day."

Tasha walked out of the kitchen and went upstairs and told Amra about Damon. "You will not believe what I did today," she said as she walked into the room that she shared with Amra.

"What?"

"I saw Damon."

Amra got up off of her bed. "No, you didn't!"

Tasha put the phone in Amra's face. "Yes, I did."

Amra gave Tasha almost the exact same reaction as Honey had given her. They were all excited, not at the fact that Tasha could get a twenty-year-old, but that she had gotten him to give her his phone.

Tasha called Damon whenever she could, and that next week, he picked her up and took her and Amra to Honey's open house. He didn't know Tasha was only sixteen, figuring she'd graduated with Honey, making her at least eighteen. When he pulled up to Honey's house, he told Tasha, "Call me later, all right? I'm trying to see you tonight."

Tasha leaned over and gave him a kiss. "Okay. Thank you, Damon."

Amra and Tasha got out of the car.

Amra laughed. "It ain't even been a week, and his nose is wide open. Your pussy must be gold."

Tasha laughed, but she hadn't actually had sex with Damon. She just figured that he liked spending time with her, so he went out of his way to make her happy.

No one knew, but Tasha was still a virgin, and she had no intentions of losing that to Damon.

They walked around the house and into Honey's back yard, where her open house was being held.

"Damn, there's a lot of people here," Amra said as she maneuvered her way through the crowd to find Honey. Almost every person that had graduated with Honey was at her open house.

Honey came up to them with a plate of bar-becue ribs. "Hey, y'all. Thanks for coming," she said, smiling at her friends.

Tasha handed Honey a card and hugged her friend. "You know we wouldn't miss it. Damon gave me a hundred dollars to put in your card."

Honey smiled. "Oh, did he now?" She was amazed at how much money Tasha was getting from this dude. He was spending money on her like it grew on trees. She heard her mother call her name, and she turned to her friends and said, "Well, I have to go meet and greet, so just chill or whatever. There's some food over there. My momma's hooking it up. Y'all know that y'all can make yourselves at home."

Honey's open house was off the chain. It seemed like no one wanted to leave. It was like a party, and it lasted until well past eleven P.M.

That's basically how the whole summer went. It was one big party.

Tasha continued to see Damon, and the more she saw him, the more money, clothes, and jew-elry he gave her. It was like Christmas every day, and life was good.

Summer was about to end. There was only two weeks left, and Honey was putting the finishing touches on her plans to go to Flint. She rolled up a blunt in Amra's room.

"So, when are you leaving?" Amra asked Honey.

"Not this Tuesday coming up, but next Tuesday."

Amra shook her head, still upset that Honey was going to Flint. "That's fucked up. Flint is far as hell."

Tasha was upset too, but not at Honey, just at the circumstance. Honey had become like a sister to her. "Yeah, you better not get there and start acting all funny either, bitch. Don't be acting like you can't call us and shit."

Honey laughed. "Y'all know it ain't even like that. We sisters, and that's not gon' change just because I'm moving. I'm gon' always be here whenever you bitches need me. You know me better than that. And shit, y'all only got one more year of high school, and as soon as y'all graduate, y'all can come out there. We'll be doing it big for real. I told y'all about how those Midwest niggas get down."

Tasha could feel the tears forming in her eyes. Honey was like her sister for real, and she didn't want her to go and forget about them. *They are the only family I've got,* she thought as she looked at Amra and Honey. "Look, we got to promise to always stay in contact. We got to stay together. No matter what, after we graduate, you have to come back for us. We all got to promise each other, and we can't break this promise. You two are the only family that I got, and I ain't trying to forget about that just because Honey is moving away."

Amra nodded her head. "I promise."

"I promise," Tasha said, wiping her eyes.

Honey hugged her sisters. "I promise."

Tasha jumped up. "Hold on. Let me take a picture of us." She went into her drawer and pulled out a digital camera.

"Where you get that from?" Honey asked.

Tasha shrugged her shoulders. "Damon bought it for me."

Honey and Amra looked at each other.

Tasha ignored them and got close to her friends and held her arm out and snapped the picture herself.

Two weeks later, Honey packed her clothes and looked at the picture of her, Tasha, and Amra. *I promise,* she thought. She carefully placed it on top of all her clothes in her suitcase. She had said her good-byes to Tasha and Amra over the phone the night before. She didn't want them to go with her to the airport because she knew for sure that she wouldn't get on the plane and leave them if they were there watching her. Her mother drove her to the airport. She kissed her good-bye, and she got on a plane to Michigan.

Tasha lay in her bed staring at the picture of her and her friends. *I love you, Honey.* She knew that Honey was off to a new city, and just hoped that she would get there safely. And although a year apart was a long time, deep in her heart, she knew that Honey would not forget about them.

Amra sat in her summer school class and stared at the clock. It read 11:38. She knew Honey's plane had left at eleven, and she felt the pain in her heart as she realized that one of her best friends had just left her. She opened up her math book, and the picture that she had taken with her friends two weeks earlier fell onto the floor. She picked it up and looked at it. *You better remember,* she thought. She quickly wiped away the tear that slid down her face.

Chapter Four

As Honey boarded the plane, she thought about her friends she had just left behind. She felt guilty for leaving them, but she had to worry about herself first. She sat back in the seat on the plane, listening to her CD player.

A couple of hours later, she arrived at Flint's Bishop International Airport. She took a deep breath and got up to exit the plane. When she stepped through the gates, she noticed her aunt waiting for her, and walked toward her with a big smile. It had been a long time since she had last seen her, but her aunt still looked the same. Tammy was a woman who aged well. Though she was in her forties, she could easily pass for a lady in her mid-twenties.

Honey dropped her bags and embraced her aunt. Tammy hugged Honey, and they rocked back and forth, hugging each other. Tammy was happy to see her only niece. It had been over three years since the last time she had seen her.

She grabbed Honey by both shoulders. "Look at you . . . all grown up!"

Honey smiled. "Where's Mimi?"

Mimi was Tammy's daughter and Honey's favorite and only cousin. As children, they were inseparable, until Tammy up and moved out of town.

"She went to the bathroom about ten minutes ago. She should be walking her fast ass back any minute now."

Just as Tammy finished her sentence, Mimi started running toward Honey with her arms out. They hugged and jumped up and down screaming. People started to look at them strangely, but they didn't give a damn.

Honey noticed that Mimi's looks had changed. She remembered a skinny nappy-headed girl with braces. Mimi had cut her hair real short, and had almost no hair at all. The look was feminine, and it looked good on her. She had dyed her hair blonde and developed a body to die for. Mimi had hazel contacts, and her teeth were pretty and perfectly aligned.

"Look at you, girl. You looking good."

"You looking good too," Mimi replied.

Mimi had developed a Midwest slur, and Honey could hear it in every word. Mimi and Tammy each took one of Honey's bags and began to exit the airport.

Mimi and Honey caught up on old times and talked nonstop the whole car ride home. Mimi mentioned to Honey that there was a community college near her home that she was thinking about going to. Honey thought back to when they were younger. They'd always said that they would go to college together when they graduated.

"I guess I'll check it out sometime this summer," Honey lied. She had no intention of attending college. She was there to get on her hustle, not sit up in a classroom all day.

Mimi nodded her head in approval as Tammy pulled up to their South Side home.

Honey took a look around and noticed a group of niggas shooting dice on a stoop, kids spraying water from the fire hydrant, and some teenagers playing stickball in the street. She thought to herself, *Damn! Everybody's doing something.*

When the girls exited the car, the guys on the stoop next door stopped all their movement, all eyes glued on Honey. A couple of them tried to holler.

"Hey, ma!"

"What's yo' name, baby?"

Honey didn't even look toward them. She was surprised that the house looked so nice inside. Judging from the outside, she thought the house was raggedy-looking. The big white house sat right in the middle of the ghetto. They had black leather furniture and had a big-screen television in the living room.

Mimi and Honey walked back to Mimi's room, where Mimi helped her unpack.

Honey pulled her hair back into a ponytail. "What's really good?"

"Nothing. Trying to get out the 'hood. I need to find a baller who's trying to save a ho, you feel me?"

They both burst out into laughter and gave each other a high five.

Mimi didn't even let Honey settle before she reached under her bed and grabbed her "candy jar", as she liked to call it. As soon as she opened the black shoebox, a strong weed aroma filled the air. Mimi grabbed a blunt and some weed from the box and began to split the blunt with her fingernail. She filled the blunt with some weed and put it to her mouth and started to light it.

Honey's eyes shot open. "Girl, yo' momma in the other room!" She got up and closed the door so her aunt wouldn't see them with the blunt.

"Oh yeah, I almost forgot." Mimi opened the door and yelled, "Ma, you wanna hit this blunt?"

Tammy stepped in the room. "Hell yeah! Light it up!"

Honey was amazed. She looked at her aunt, and then back at Mimi, and thought to herself, *Hell nah!*

Tammy passed the blunt to Honey, and Honey puffed away. Tammy left their smoke session after half of the blunt was gone, and Mimi and Honey continued their "puff, puff, give" rotation.

Mimi got up and turned up the radio, and Jay-Z's latest song began to play. The girls just sat back and bounced to the music.

After the spliff had burned to its end, Mimi reached under her bed for the candy jar, and her phone rang. The vibration of Mimi's cell phone startled her, and she jumped. Honey started to laugh out loud, and Mimi joined her in the laughter. Mimi put her finger over her mouth to signal Honey to hush and answered the phone. Honey went to the bathroom as Mimi began to talk on the phone.

When Honey returned, Mimi was searching through the closet for an outfit. "Find something to wear. We're going out tonight. Mama said we can use her car tonight."

Honey agreed, but mentioned that she was tired from her flight and wanted to take a nap. She lay in the other bed in Mimi's room and went to sleep.

As the girls began to get dressed and do their hair, Mimi's phone rang. She answered it and paused for a minute. Then she yelled into the phone, "Stop fucking calling me! I told you, I can't fuck with you no more. It's over!" She folded her phone up and took a deep breath.

Honey smiled. "Girl, you okay?"

"Yeah, but that nigga won't stop calling a bitch. I quit that nigga a month ago, and he still on my ass."

Honey started to brush her hair, stroking it slowly.

"B, I wish I had your hair."

"Girl, please. I wish I had your body."

Both of them began to chuckle.

Mimi interrupted the laughter. "Oh shit, it's time to go. It's ten thirty." Mimi grabbed her jacket and they headed for the club. She wanted to show Honey around Flint, and if she was anything like her cousin, the first place she would want to go to is the club.

They got out of the car and stood in line so they could enter the club.

Honey looked up toward the front of the line. "Damn, girl! This mu'fucka is packed. This line is way too long."

Just as Honey finished her sentence, a bouncer screamed, "Mimi!"

Mimi looked at the front of the line and yelled back, "Jay!" She pulled Honey by the hand and headed toward the front of the line. When they approached the bouncer, Mimi gave him a big hug. "She's with me." Mimi pointed at Honey.

The bouncer opened the doors for them, and they went into the club. Honey was impressed and gave Mimi a high five as they entered the building. The club was packed, and everyone was dancing, drinking, and having a good time. As soon as they walked in, people started yelling, "Mimi!" Mimi started nodding at people. "What up, Mimi, baby?" It seemed like everybody had a different nickname for her.

The girls went toward a table near the back of the club, sat down, and ordered two drinks.

Honey looked over at Mimi. "It's jumping in here."

Mimi was bouncing to the music. "Yeah, it's always hype in here. This is my spot. Let's go and dance."

They both got up and walked to the dance floor and began to dance with each other. Before long, a dude cut in and began to dance with Mimi, and another guy got on Honey.

After three songs Honey stopped dancing and went toward the table where they had been sitting. Mimi noticed Honey leave the dance floor and followed her back to the table. Both girls were lightly sweating.

Honey said, "I'm about to go to the bathroom to freshen up. Where is it?"

Mimi stood up. "Over here. I'll go with you."

They entered the bathroom, and both of them went straight to the sink.

Honey brushed her hair while looking in the mirror. She laughed. "That nigga I was dancing with was starting to get musty. I was like, hell nah! I hurried up and left his ass on the dance floor."

Mimi leaned toward Honey and sniffed her.

Honey leaned back. "Bitch, what you doing?"

"I was just checking to see if that nigga stench got on you." Mimi laughed loudly.

Honey started to laugh. "Girl, please. Don't nothing on my body stink."

Mimi told Honey she had to pee and entered the stall. Then two girls came in the bathroom talking loudly.

Honey looked at them through the mirror and noticed that they were wearing braids and big hoop earrings. They both were 'hood rat-looking girls. They stood at the sink next to the mirror Honey was standing in front of and began to talk. One of them said, "Girl, you see all these niggas in here? I'm getting me a baller tonight. Watch me."

The other girl was in the mirror putting on lip liner. She pursed her lips together. "Fuck the niggas! Did you see that bitch, Mimi in here? I should beat that bitch ass! She think she's the shit. Her stank ass ain't nothing but a ho. I know if that bitch calls my nigga one more time, we gon' go at it."

Honey stopped putting on her eyeliner and looked over at the girls, but they were so busy talking, they didn't notice her. The two girls exited the bathroom, and Mimi came out of the stall. "Did you hear those bitches?" Honey asked.

Mimi took off her earrings. "Yeah, I heard them hoes."

Mimi wasn't the one to be played with. She never had beef with anyone for too long before acting on it. She walked around the club looking for the girls who were talking shit about her in the bathroom. Though she hadn't seen them, she already knew who they were. Honey followed her, knowing they were about to get down.

They spotted the girls sitting at the bar, and Mimi immediately made her way over to them. She walked past them with an attitude and sat right next to them. Honey didn't go near them. She just sat back and watched to see what Mimi was going to do. Next thing you know, Mimi was fighting both of the chicks. One of the girls was on the floor wrestling with Mimi, and the other one was kicking her in the side. Honey rushed over to the bar and hit the girl standing up with full force, her rings digging deep into her knuckles as her fist collided with the girl's mouth. The girl fell to the floor, and out of instinct, Honey knelt down next to her, grabbed her hair, and dragged her around the club, hitting her hard in the face as she went. "Bitch!" She gave the girl an asswhupping she wouldn't forget.

The people in the club gathered around to watch the fight. Someone yelled, "Damn! She is beating her ass!"

Honey stomped the girl hard, and then felt strong arms grab her and pull her off the girl sprawled out on the floor. The girl got up off the floor and lunged at Honey, but someone grabbed her and held her back. Honey managed to wiggle away from the bouncer that was holding her and ran up on the girl and bust her hard in face. The girl fell to the floor, and the bouncers rushed to her aid to see if she was okay. Honey looked over at Mimi and saw that she was on top of the other girl, beating the shit out of her. She ran over to the bar, grabbed a beer bottle off of the counter and smashed it in the girl's face. The girl grabbed her face as the blood dripped from her forehead, and Honey and Mimi both kicked the girl in the face repeatedly.

Mimi got up first and noticed that the other girl was knocked out. She grabbed Honey and said, "Let's get the fuck out of here." They had beat the girls down so badly, Mimi knew if they stuck around, they would be spending the night downtown.

"I hate that stupid-ass bitch! She had the nerve to talk shit about me? That's why I beat her ass," Mimi said.

Honey had no clue why they were fighting. The only reason she'd jumped in was because Mimi was her cousin. She looked at her swollen knuckles, shaking her hands to stop them from throbbing. "Who in the hell were they?"

Mimi shrugged her shoulders. "These nobody-ass bitches named Keesha and her friend Kia. We been beefing since high school. They're jealous of me, and always trying to jump somebody. I started fucking with Kia's man about a month or so ago, and ever since then, it's been beef every time we see each other. It ain't my fault she can't keep her man."

"Shit! Let me know when you about to scrap. I didn't know what you was about to do."

"Sorry. You know how it is when you on a mission. I saw you over there beating her ass though. Your ass fight like a nigga," Mimi said.

They both laughed and entered the car.

"Damn! Those bitches done fucked up my night. If Tasha and Amra were here, they would have really felt it." Honey put her hands on her hips.

Mimi frowned. "Who are they?"

Honey laughed to herself. "Oh, they just my girls from back home. They cool as hell, and they always got my back."

Mimi reached out her hand. "Thanks for having my back, girl."

Honey replied, "You know I got yo' back, girl. We family. Fuck them hoes! If they want it again, then they know where to find us."

When they arrived at the house, Mimi put the car in park. "Honey, you my girl, you know that?"

Honey nodded her head yes, and gave her a wink. Mimi turned back the ignition, and they began to listen to her Lauryn Hill CD.

Mimi reached in her purse and pulled out some weed. She rolled a blunt and sparked it.

"Damn, bitch! I thought I smoked a lot!"

Mimi giggled. "After fighting those hoes at the club, I need one."

The girls sat there, smoking and reminiscing about their childhood, and how they would get out of the ghetto.

"Where do you see yourself in five years?" Mimi asked.

"I'm going to have a big-ass salon with a Lex-us—paid for, not leased. I can't wait until I can sit back in my own shit, you know? Just chill and enjoy life and sit back and count my own money, not money that a nigga done gave me, but my own shit." Honey looked at Mimi to see if she could relate. "You feel me?"

"Hell yeah. That's what's up." Mimi always thought about get-rich-quick schemes and was always on the look out for that big lick. She was what you called ghetto fabulous. She had grown up in the 'hood, knew all the right people, and was determined to be paid within the next five years.

That next morning around eleven o'clock, Honey awoke before anyone else. She realized she hadn't talked to her girls in a while, so she called Tasha's cell phone. When she got no answer, she left a message: "Tasha, where the hell is you and Amra at? This is Honey. I miss you, girl. Call me."

Honey went to the bathroom to brush her teeth. She began to brush her teeth and saw a man pass the bathroom, startling her. Her aunt Tammy followed him, and they headed toward the door, never noticing Honey in the bathroom. Honey overheard their conversation and began to eavesdrop.

"How much do I owe you?" the man asked.

"Two hundred, baby! This pussy is well worth two bills."

Honey heard the shuffling of paper and assumed it was money being peeled off. *Damn! Aunt Tammy's tricking? That's how their house is so plush and shit. She doesn't work, and she ain't on welfare. Fuck that! She out cold!*

Tammy snapped Honey out her thoughts. "Hey, Honey. I didn't know you were up. Want some eggs?"

Honey thought about where her aunt's hands might have been. "No thanks, Aunt Tammy. I'm not that hungry."

Tammy smiled. "Okay, baby." Then she walked into the kitchen and began to cook breakfast.

Honey shook her head and continued to brush her teeth. *Fuck that!*

Chapter Five

Tasha and Amra returned to school a week after Honey had left for the Midwest. "It feels funny being here without Honey," Amra said as she walked with Tasha down the hallways of their school. Everything seemed different. Instead of a trio, they were now a pair.

"I know, shit ain't the same. At least she called to let us know that she made it there safely."

Tasha and Amra parted ways, and Tasha headed to her homeroom. She knew her senior year would go by quickly, so she wasn't stressing it. She had taken most of her required classes during her other years, so she only needed to take three classes. Tasha was focused on graduating from high school. Her grades were good, and she wanted to keep them that way, to secure a good future. She hadn't really thought about what her future had in store for her, but she wanted to have a better life. She wanted to go to Flint after high school, but after that, she had no clue. *Maybe I'll go to college,* she thought to herself.

At lunchtime, Tasha and Amra sat down at a table.

"I hate school." Amra said, and bit into the cold fries that the cafeteria served.

"Just stay on your shit this year so that you will graduate," Tasha said, reminding her friend of her stint in summer school.

Amra wasn't trying to hear that though. "So, you want to come to this little get-together with me Saturday night?"

Tasha nodded her head. "You know I'm coming with you. Who's having it?"

"Oh, this nigga name Tariq. I got his number over the summer. He invited me to a little party at his house."

Tasha was down to go. She'd been partying over the whole summer, so she figured going to the party tomorrow wouldn't hurt.

Saturday came, and Tasha called Damon to tell him she was chilling with Amra for the weekend. He'd gotten used to seeing her every weekend and sounded disappointed, but Tasha didn't care. *That nigga getting too attached anyway. I hope he knows we're just friends.*

Tasha looked in the mirror in the room and turned around to make sure her panty line wasn't showing. She had on a red dress that slit open at the top to show a little cleavage. She knew that she would be fresh to death when she put it on.

Amra came out of the bathroom wearing tight white pants with a white sleeveless shirt that barely covered her breasts.

Tasha applied bronzer to her already brown face. "When is your boy coming to pick us up?"

Amra looked at her cell phone. "It's eight fifteen. He'll be here at nine."

Tasha put on some gloss and shook her head to drop the curls she had put in. "It always looks better when Honey does it," she mumbled to herself as she looked in the mirror. Tasha's cell phone rang and she answered it, "Hello," she answered, still shaking her head, trying to make the curls fall.

Damon said, "Can I see you tonight?"

Tasha frowned. "I told you I was chilling with my girl tonight, so I'm gon' have to catch up with you another time."

Damon smacked his lips and said, "What about after you done chilling with your girl? Can I come and get you?" He asked her in almost a pleading way.

Tasha shook her head. *Damn, nigga, I said no.* "It's probably gon' be late, so I'm not gon' be able to."

After another ten minutes of negotiating, Damon finally accepted the fact that he would not be seeing her tonight, and Tasha hung up the phone.

Amra got a call on her phone. "We on our way," she said before hanging up. "Come on, they're in the driveway." They grabbed their purses and were out the door. They walked down the driveway and got into the Tahoe parked in front of their yard.

"Hey, this is my sister, Tasha. Tasha, this is my friend, Tariq."

Tasha shook his hand and sat back in the back seat.

They drove into Brooklyn and pulled up to a nice two-story brick home. Tasha knew that whoever owned the house wasn't broke. She got out of the car, shook her hair making sure it was loose, and followed Amra and Tariq into the house.

There was haze in the air when they walked in the house. People were lighting up blunts all over the house, shooting dice, playing cards, and just chilling. And the music was crunk.

Tasha relaxed. She usually didn't feel comfortable in house parties, but this one was under control.

Tariq fell into the scene of the party, and Amra and Tasha sat down in one of the chairs in the front of the house. Somebody passed around a blunt, and Amra hit it a couple times. She seemed to relax easily after she smoked, and this time was no different.

Tariq came back with a tall, basketball-player type. He pointed to Tasha. "Tasha, this is my nigga, Joe."

Tasha smiled and shook his hand. She looked him up and down and could tell he had a little bit of money in his pockets. He wasn't bad in the looks department either. The nigga was fine as hell. "So, is this your house?" she asked, screaming over the music.

He nodded his head. "Just a little something to start out with."

Tasha looked around and noticed the plasma TV and the black furniture. *It seems like quite a bit to me.*

Joe led Tasha to one of the less crowded rooms, and she immediately became uncomfortable. He looked at her and said, "So, how old are you, Miss Tasha?"

Tasha looked at him. "Seventeen, and cut the *miss*—I don't fall for games."

Joe laughed, rubbing his goatee. "Okay, okay. That's good, 'cuz I don't play them."

Tasha looked Joe in the eye. *Witty mu'fucka!*

"You want something to drink?"

She shook her head no. "That's okay. I don't drink. I do want to shoot some dice though." Tasha didn't know how to shoot craps. She was just looking for an excuse to get out of the secluded room.

Joe smiled, grabbed her hand, and led her to the living room, where a group of dudes were in the middle of a dice game. He pulled a wad of money out of his baggy jeans and peeled off one of the fifties. He put it in the air. "You know how to shoot?"

Tasha rolled her eyes. "Yeah, I know how to shoot."

He handed her the money and she got into the game. Not knowing what she was doing, Tasha quickly lost his money, but Joe didn't seem to care, because he kept peeling off twenty-dollar bills for her to shoot with.

Finally, Tasha got tired of losing money, so she gave up. She turned to Joe and said, "Sorry."

Joe smiled sexily. "It's okay, ma. Let me show you how to shoot." He pulled out a twenty, laid it on the ground, and then picked up the dice. "You got to blow the dice, baby."

Tasha laughed. She blew on the dice that Joe held up to her lips. He threw the dice and one landed on a four and the other on a three. "Seven means you win."

Tasha laughed. "I must be good luck."

"You must be."

Joe collected his money and got up from the game. He and Tasha found Tariq and Amra, and they all chilled until the party was over.

Joe walked Tasha out to Tariq's car. He asked, "Do you mind if I take you to the crib?"

Tasha shook her head no, and they walked over to a freshly painted candy red '84 Cutlass Supreme on spinners. He opened her door for her, and she got in.

Damn, this car is too fly! Tasha thought to herself while Joe walked around the car. He had a PlayStation 3, a DVD player, and a TV hooked up in the car. She couldn't believe how good the old car looked.

Joe took Tasha home, and they sat in front of the house talking for about an hour. He put in a DVD, and they laughed while watching the legendary 'hood movie, *Friday*. She was enjoying Joe and was happy she had gone to the party. He was cool people.

Her cell phone rang, and the caller ID said Damon. She didn't answer it, but the call ruined the moment. She turned off her phone. "Well, I better go."

Joe rubbed his chin. "That was your nigga, huh?"

Tasha laughed. "I don't have a man. Niggas can't keep tabs on me."

Joe nodded his head and smiled as Tasha stared at him. They just looked at each other, and Tasha blushed, feeling awkward for staring so hard. *He is so fine!* she thought to herself. She couldn't help it though. Joe was mysterious, and something about him kept her eye.

"I got to go." Tasha opened her door and climbed out. Halfway up the driveway, she turned back and walked over to his side of the car. She unclipped Joe's cell phone from his belt and entered her number into it. "Make sure you use this." When she clipped his phone back on his belt, she felt hard metal near his waistline and knew it was a gun. It kind of scared her a little bit because she had never actually seen a gun up close.

Joe could see that she was shaken, so he grabbed her hand softly and kissed her wrist. He started his car and pulled off.

As soon as he left, Amra and Tariq pulled up. Amra jumped out of the car, and Tariq pulled off. She approached Tasha. "Where the hell did you and Joe go?" she asked in a teasing way.

"Nowhere, so get yo' mind out the gutter. I been here for a couple hours. Where did you and Tariq go, is the question."

Amra pulled out some money. "This is what I was doing—making money."

Tasha could tell that Amra was high as a kite, so she led her friend up to their room, and they went to sleep before Ms. Pat came in to see if they were all right.

Tasha loved Sundays. All she did was chill and watch *Lifetime*. After waking up and eating one of Ms. Pat's big Sunday breakfasts, she checked the messages on her phone. *Damn, three missed calls!* She dialed her voice mail and hit the button to play her messages.

First Message: *"What up, girl? This is Damon. Call me when you get this."*

Second Message: *"Tasha, where the hell is you and Amra at? This is Honey. I miss you, girl. Call me."*

When Tasha heard Honey's voice, she immediately became excited. *Damn! How did I miss that call? We miss you too.* She made a mental note to call her back, and then continued to check her messages.

Third Message: *"Tasha, this is Damon. Where the fuck you at? It's two in the morning. Why you ain't answering my calls? You better not still be out!"*

Tasha had never had anyone tell her what she could and could not do, and she for damn sure wasn't about to let Damon start. *I better not? What the fuck is wrong with this nigga? Why the hell is he calling me, trying to trip, and check me about what I'm doing? I told his ass that I was going out, and that's that. I don't have to explain shit to him. I ain't got no daddy. He must be out his damn mind. He ain't even my man. I'm gon' have to let his ass know.*

Tasha went upstairs to find Amra. She stormed into the room. "Let me tell you what Damon's ass gon' leave on my voice mail—"

Amra was on her cell phone, so she held up her finger to signal for Tasha to wait. "A'ight, I said I'm gon' tell her. Dang! Is that all you called me for? Okay, bye." Amra looked at Tasha and smiled. "That was Tariq. He told me to tell you that Joe wants to see you tonight."

Tasha forgot all about Damon. "For real?" She liked Joe, but she wasn't expecting to see him again. She walked out of the room and called Joe.

Joe answered on the third ring. "Yeah?"

Tasha recognized his sexy voice as soon as he picked up the phone, and smiled. "This is Tasha."

Joe wasn't expecting her call, but was glad to hear from her. "I was just talking about you, ma," he said, trying to blow up Tasha's head. It was working too, because she was feeling him.

"Oh, really! You were talking about me? Damn! Why you got me all on the brain?" she asked, flirting with him.

He laughed. "Yeah, I was thinking about you. Don't get the big head. So, when you gon' come see me, you know, without all the people around and shit?"

Tasha wanted to see Joe, but she didn't want it to seem like she was jockeying him. "I don't know. You tell me."

"Tonight."

Joe stepped out of the car in jeans and a white T-shirt with some crispy Force One's. He approached Tasha and hugged her when he got close. He gently grabbed her chin and kissed her, and she kissed him back, knowing he wanted to kiss her the other night. Tasha felt Joe's gun in his waistline, and that made her stop.

They went to eat. When the waiter came, she ordered a salad. Joe frowned at her.

"What you looking at?"

Joe shook his head. "I know you ain't get all that ass from eating salad. You don't got to be cute, ma. You already got me interested. I want you to have dinner with me."

Tasha laughed when Joe told the waiter to bring them out two steaks. She liked him. He was real and didn't try to beat around the bush. He said what he thought and didn't hold his tongue. Joe made her laugh, and she found his thuggish way attractive.

Tasha's phone rang. It was Damon, so she let it ring.

I don't feel like dealing with his ass right now.

When she got home, Damon called her again. "Hello?" she answered in a frustrated tone.

"Why you ain't get at me when I called you?"

Tasha didn't feel that she had to explain herself to anybody. "I was busy. I told you I was gon' be with Amra this whole weekend."

"Well, what you doing now?"

Tasha sighed. "I'm about to go to bed. I have school tomorrow." Tasha hung up with Damon and made a mental note, *I'm going to cut this nigga off as soon as possible. He's getting a little bit too crazy for me.*

Tasha went through school each week, ignoring Damon's phone calls and accepting more of Joe's. Joe was different than all the other chumps she was used to hustling. He didn't fall for her game. It wasn't about the money with him. He hadn't bought her a single thing since she'd met him. She just enjoyed being around him and was really feeling him.

As the school year continued to fly by, Amra grew tired of school by the day. She became more and more restless. She had quickly stopped fucking with Tariq and was officially ready to experience the Midwest. *It's time to see what a new city has to offer.* She wasn't just ready to party in Flint, though. She missed Honey too, and was ready for the clique to be back together again. *I'm tired of this shit,* she thought to herself, thinking about the tedious schedule of school. She didn't want to tell her momma and Tasha, but it was clear she wasn't going to graduate. *I might as well have dropped out a long time ago. School ain't for everybody anyway. Shit! It definitely ain't for me. Everybody can't be an A student like Tasha.*

Amra walked out of the school and saw Joe waiting there to pick her and Tasha up. Tasha was already in the car, so she walked over and got in.

"What up, Amra?" Joe said.

"What's good, Joe?"

Amra thought about her future as she sat in the back seat of Joe's Cutlass. There was only a month left before graduation, and she had to tell her mother the bad news soon.

When they pulled up in front of Ms. Pat's house, Amra saw Damon's Escalade parked on the corner.

She knew Tasha was too busy with Joe to notice the car, so she sent her a text message on her phone reading: *Damon is sitting at the corner. Look!*

Tasha's eyes got bucked as she thought about what she would say to him. She had been avoiding him for months, but he still hadn't gotten the picture. She said, "Um, Joe, I got to go. I'll call you later, okay?" She fidgeted with his car door and got out, trying to rush into the house before Damon could confront her. Just as she looked up, she saw Damon approach Joe's car. "Shit!"

Amra jumped out, and so did Joe.

Damon screamed at Tasha. "What the fuck is you doing riding with this nigga?"

"What are you yelling for? Don't be coming over to my damn house causing no drama. I am not your chick."

Joe walked over and stood beside Tasha, and put his arm around her. "What the fuck is up?" he asked, standing toe to toe with Damon. Joe lifted his shirt and showed Damon his gun.

Damon realized he had come unprepared. He looked at Tasha. "Fuck it!" he said, walking away. "We gon' handle this later."

Joe turned to Tasha. "What the fuck was that? That's your man?"

Tasha didn't have time for another nigga to be trying to check her. She walked away shaking her head, and then disappeared into the house with Amra right behind her.

After that little situation, Tasha stopped fucking with Damon and barely felt like dealing with Joe. She liked Joe a lot, but she didn't know if she was ready for what he was ready for. It was obvious that he wanted her to be more than just a friend, and Tasha felt she was too young to be tied down. She wanted to do what she wanted to do without having to explain herself to anyone. She knew that Joe wasn't like Damon. He wouldn't take any bullshit, and she didn't want to disrespect him by even assuming that he should. She still talked to Joe sometimes, but she was focusing on her graduation and decided to keep things with him on a friendly level.

A couple of weeks before graduation, Ms. Pat came into Amra and Tasha's room and said, "Have you girls picked out something to wear to graduation yet? You've got to let me know, so I can give you the money to go buy it."

"I got to talk to you about that, Ma. You too, Tasha." Amra sat on the edge of her bed.

Ms. Pat and Tasha were all ears as they focused their attention on Amra.

"I'm not graduating," she said, her eyes down.

"What!" Ms. Pat said, "What do you mean, you are not graduating?"

Tasha was in disbelief. *I knew that she didn't like school, but I didn't know that she was failing.*

Ms. Pat just shook her head. "You know what? You are about to be eighteen. You both are. Now Tasha has a future, but you . . . I don't know. It's in your own hands now. But I'll tell you one thing. You are not about to be living up in here for free if you ain't going to school, so after graduation, let me know what it's going to be." With those words, Ms. Pat left the room.

Tasha looked at Amra. "I'm sorry, Amra. Don't worry about that shit. You can get your GED."

Amra appreciated Tasha's understanding and support. She knew she had fucked up, and the last thing she needed was someone telling her how bad her life was going to be.

Three weeks later, Tasha sat on the football field in her white cap and gown. *I can't believe I made it! I'm finally here!*

"Tasha Parks."

Tasha heard her name being called, and she stood up to get her diploma. She walked across the stage and heard applause from the crowd. It was truly the proudest moment in her life.

After the ceremony, she walked over to Amra, who had tears in her eyes. Even though Amra did not share the stage with Tasha, she was still proud of her friend's accomplishment. "Congratulations!" she said as she gave Tasha a hug. "I have a surprise for you, so close your eyes."

Tasha put one hand over her eyes.

"Okay, you can look."

She turned around expecting to see flowers or some type of gift, but instead, she saw Honey looking as beautiful as ever. "Oh my God! B!" Tasha screamed as she jumped up and down with her friend.

Honey hugged Tasha. "Yo', it's been a long time. You did it, girl! You graduated! You ready to leave this stankin'-ass city alone? I told you I was gon' keep my promise."

Amra joined their circle. "She came over right after you left this morning. I didn't even know she was coming."

Tasha looked at Honey. She looked good. She had cut her hair in long layers, and her Chloe glasses matched her black outfit.

Amra, Tasha, and Honey went back to Ms. Pat's house, where Honey pulled out two plane tickets. "Y'all bitches ready?"

Amra looked confused. "We leaving tonight?"

Honey smiled. "Yeah, bitches, we leaving tonight. Let's go. Get your shit."

Amra and Tasha were so geeked to be leaving home, they started jumping up and down. They had been waiting for a year to join Honey there.

"What are we gon' tell Ms. Pat?"

Amra's mom had been upset at her since she had told her about not graduating. "I don't care what you tell her. I ain't telling her shit. She ain't here, so we'll leave a note. She wants me out of her house anyway, so I'm out."

Tasha agreed to leave, but she felt bad about just leaving a note for Ms. Pat. She went into the kitchen, grabbed a piece of paper, and started writing:

Dear Ms. Pat,

I love you. For as long as I can remember, you have always been here for me. You are like my mother, and you are the only person who cared about me when my own mother did not. You have taken care of me, put clothes on my back, and food in my stomach, and I want to tell you thank you from the bottom of my heart. Thank you for everything, Ms. Pat. I love you dearly.

Amra and I are going to Michigan with Honey tonight. Amra is upset, so she wanted to leave right away. I just wanted to let you know that we will be okay, and to let you know that I love you, and so does she.

Sincerely, Tasha

Tasha folded the letter and placed it on top of Ms. Pat's pillow. She finished packing her clothes, and then called Joe when she was finished. She didn't feel like she owed him an explanation, but she still wanted to let him know she was leaving.

"Hello?" Tasha smiled at the sound of his voice. "Can you come over here?" Joe said yes, and within fifteen minutes, he was at her door.

Honey saw Joe get out of his car. She leaned over to Amra and whispered, "Who is that?"

Amra laughed. "His name is Joe. That nigga fine, ain't he?"

"Hell yeah. Tasha done stepped her game up." Honey nodded her head in approval.

Tasha walked outside with Joe. She looked at him sadly as she gave him a hug.

"You look good, ma," he said as he stood in front of her and stared down at her. "Why didn't you tell me you were graduating today? I would've done something special for you."

She looked up at Joe and couldn't help but smile. When she was around him, he made her heart melt. She was feeling this dude. "I guess I didn't think you would come."

"I'm proud of you, ma. That's a good look right there. Everybody don't make it through high school. I would've showed up."

Tasha shifted in her stance. "I just wanted to tell you bye before I leave."

Joe frowned in confusion. "What you mean, before you leave? Where are you going?"

Tasha put her hands in her back pockets. "I'm moving to Flint, Michigan."

Joe nodded his head and just looked at Tasha.

Tasha was searching for anything in his eyes that showed how he felt. Joe never showed his emotions. *Just tell me you want me to stay. Just say it, Joe.*

Joe went into his pocket and pulled out a wad of money. He counted out a thousand dollars and handed it to her. It was the first time he had given her anything.

Tasha didn't take it, though. She honestly liked Joe and wasn't trying to get him for his money.

Joe folded the money up anyway and put it in her purse. "Take it. You don't know what Flint's like. I got people out that way. That city is the gutter. You might need it."

Joe put his hand on her chin and kissed her. His hands wrapped around her waist and rested on her ass as he kissed her softly. His warm lips sent tingles down her spine as she stood on her tiptoes to come to his height. "Take care of yourself, Tasha." He kissed her lips softly one last time, and walked away from her.

Tasha didn't know what to feel. Her heart was racing, and she didn't know if she should stop him from leaving or not. She didn't know that she felt this way about him until it was time for her to tell him good-bye. *Do I love him?* she asked herself, trying to figure it out before he left. Before she could make sense of her feelings, Joe got into his car and pulled away without looking back. "Bye!" she said quietly. She felt her heart break for the first time. She slowly turned around. *Am I doing the right thing?* she thought to herself as she looked at Honey and Amra.

Honey and Amra packed the bags into the cab that had arrived in front of Ms. Pat's house. They got in as Tasha stood outside the house, wondering if she was making the right decision. Amra shouted from the back seat of the cab. "Tash, are you ready?"

Tasha looked at the cab, and then at the taillights of Joe's car as he drove away. She took a deep breath. "Yeah, let's go."

Chapter Six

They arrived in Flint at one o'clock in the morning. Amra was excited to be there, to be away from New York. She was anxious to hit the hottest spots in the city. Tasha was confused, not knowing what to expect from the streets of Flint.

"Mimi should be here," Honey said, leading the way through the airport.

The girls walked outside and saw a honey-colored girl with a short haircut that had been died blonde. She had hailed a cab and was standing on the outside of it. She reminded Tasha of one of the girls from a video or something. They walked up to the girl.

Honey said, "Amra, Tasha, this is my cousin, Mimi."

Mimi was thick as hell. An average-looking girl, her face wasn't all that, but she was well endowed, and her ass made up for the features she lacked.

Mimi smiled and greeted the girls. "Hey, let me get some of them bags." She helped them put their bags into the trunk, then they all got into the cab.

After a twenty-minute ride to Flint's South Side, they finally arrived at the house. When they walked in, Tasha immediately recognized the smell of weed. The pungent smell was heavy in the house.

"Hey, my babies!" a woman loudly said as she approached them all.

"This is my moms," Mimi said.

"Just call me Tammy," Mimi's mother said with a strong Midwest slur. Tammy had an old Stephanie Mills song playing loudly through the house, and she was grooving with her hands in the air. A small glass of Rémy Martin with ice was on the table as Tammy smoothly danced by herself.

Tasha smiled at Mimi's mother and introduced herself. "I'm Tasha."

"And I'm Amra."

Tammy gave both girls a friendly smile. "Okay, now I need to set some ground rules."

Tasha and Amra looked at each other with skeptical looks on their faces.

Tammy put her hands on her hips. "Now, y'all some grown women, so I'm not gonna try to tell y'all where you can and can not go. All I want is one hundred dollars apiece every month. Hell, with five of us in the house, the bills are gonna be sky-high. The money will help pay some of them and buy groceries for all of us." She paused for a minute to get the girls' reactions, but when they just nodded their heads in agreement, she added, "Well, go make yourselves at home."

After the brief introduction, Mimi led the way upstairs. The house had three bedrooms, so there was plenty of room for the girls. "This is where y'all gon' sleep." Mimi pointed into the room.

They all went in, and Tasha and Amra started to unpack.

"So, who was that nigga that you called over before we left home?" Honey asked, intrigued by Joe. Honey liked to deal with thugs. Joe's car, his clothes, the tattoos that covered his solid body, and the gun she saw through the imprint of his white T-shirt told her all she needed to know.

Tasha smiled at the thought of Joe. "That was this dude named Joe." She kept it short because she didn't want Honey to be too interested in her man. *What the fuck is she so interested for anyway?* A streak of jealousy quickly passed through her.

Mimi sat down on the bed that Tasha had chosen to sleep in. "So, what's up for tonight? I know y'all bitches didn't come here to sit in the house."

Tasha frowned at the term. *She better watch that "bitch" shit. We ain't cool like that yet.*

Amra laughed it off. "Hell nah. I didn't come here to sit in the house."

"Well look, I'm about to get dressed," Honey got up and said. "So let me know when y'all ready to go."

Mimi followed closely behind her. "Me too. I got to do my hair."

"Damn, Tasha! I can not believe we are so far away from home. On our own too, I mean, besides Tammy and all, but she doesn't count, because it don't even seem like she gon' be tripping," Amra said, playing in her own hair.

"Yeah, she's cool."

Tasha grabbed hangers from out of the closet to put her clothes up. She was tired and wasn't really in the mood to go clubbing. She had a lot on her mind, and she also wanted to call Ms. Pat to make sure she had gotten the letter.

Tasha walked out of her new room and down the hall into Honey and Mimi's room. She softly knocked before she entered, "Hey," she said as she walked in and sat on Honey's bed.

Mimi was rummaging through her closet, trying to find something to wear, and Honey was in the mirror, getting ready to do her hair.

Honey turned and looked at Tasha and immediately knew she wasn't up to going out. "Hey, we don't have to go out tonight. We can just chill if you are too tired." She walked over to her dresser and pulled some pajamas out. She already knew Tasha would take her up on her offer.

"Good. I really don't feel like partying hard tonight anyway. I have to call back home to check on Amra's mom."

Honey nodded her head and looked skeptically at Mimi.

Mimi smacked her lips and shot Honey a look that said she wasn't having it. She quickly replied, "Oh, bitch, you already know I'm going out. It's two-dollar Tuesday, and the club is going to be packed tonight. I will be in there. But don't trip, we can all do something tomorrow, or whenever y'all feel up to it."

Tasha walked back into her room and saw Amra asleep on her bed. She walked over to her and nudged her softly. Amra didn't move, so Tasha pulled the cover over her friend and turned out the lights.

Tasha picked up her cell phone and called Ms. Pat. The phone rang a couple times, and with each ring, more butterflies accumulated in her stomach.

"Hello?" Ms. Pat finally answered.

Tasha paused when she heard Ms. Pat's voice. *I hope she's not mad at us.* Tasha said nervously, "Hey, Ms. Pat—"

"Oh, thank you, Jesus! Tasha, I am so glad you called. What in the world were you girls thinking, running off to Michigan without even waiting to tell me? Where is Amra?" she yelled sternly through the phone.

Tasha could hear the anger and sadness in her voice as she spoke. "She's asleep. I'm sorry, Ms. Pat. It was wrong for us to just leave, but we're okay. We're staying with Honey's auntie for now," she explained, hoping that it would ease Ms. Pat. When there was silence, Tasha knew Ms. Pat was disappointed.

"I know you two are grown now, and I can't dictate what you two do, but you take care of my baby. Watch out for her. You and Amra are like sisters, and I love you like you are my own. Make sure you both are careful. Flint is a bad city. Don't get caught up in any mess."

"We won't. We're okay though. I don't want you to worry."

Ms. Pat was unsure about the whole situation, but she knew that the girls had their hearts and minds set. "I'm going to worry. My girls are far away from me. I know you will make smart choices, for yourself, and for Amra. That makes me feel a little better. You make sure you call me at least once a week."

Tasha felt like a big weight had been lifted off of her shoulders. She hung up the phone and went back into Honey's room.

Mimi had finished getting dressed and was getting ready to walk out the door. She looked at Tasha, and tried to convince her that she was missing out. "Are you sure you don't want to come? It's gonna be jumping."

Tasha shook her head. "Nah, I'm cool."

Mimi shrugged. "Okay," she said, and walked out of the room and headed for the club.

Honey and Tasha sat up talking, catching up on the year that had just passed. Away from each other for months, their friendship hadn't missed a beat. They were still as close as ever. The absence had made them grow fonder of each other. They sat up watching TV, eating pizza, and talking about everything they had missed in each other's life. Tasha was happy to be around her friend again.

"So, what is Mimi like?" Tasha asked Honey. Mimi seemed cool, but Honey would tell her the real deal, no matter what.

"Mimi's cool. We've been tight ever since we were babies. She's real though; she don't put up with bullshit. If y'all cool, then she will be the best friend you will ever have. But if y'all enemies, she will be the worst enemy too. That's just how she is, you know? You don't have to worry about Mimi though. Y'all will be cool."

Tasha knew that if Honey thought highly of her cousin, then she must be okay.

Tasha went into her room and tried to go to sleep. It took her a couple hours to get comfortable. Just as she was about to fall into a deep sleep, she was interrupted by the sound of Mimi shouting.

"Honey!" Mimi yelled in a slurred voice.

Tasha put her pillow over her head, trying to ignore the noise. When she heard a loud thud followed by glass breaking, she suspected that Mimi had fallen, stumbling around the dark house. She assumed that Mimi was drunk and tried to block out the noise. Then she heard Mimi fall and hit the floor hard.

Tasha jumped out of bed and ran into the hall. She turned on the hall light and saw Mimi lying on the floor, breathing hard, almost gasping for air. Blood was running onto the carpet from the cuts on her face. She ran over to Mimi. "Oh my God! What happened to you?" She tried to help Mimi up.

Mimi screamed in pain when Tasha tried to move her.

Amra appeared at the entrance to their bedroom and groggily rubbed her eyes.

"Go get Honey!" Tasha screamed.

Amra snapped awake when she saw Mimi lying on the floor. "Damn! What happened to her?"

Tasha waved her hand. "Go get Honey!"

While Amra rushed into Honey's room, Tasha pulled off Mimi's blood-soaked shirt and saw a deep cut on her stomach. She immediately ran into the bathroom and started to run cold water in the sink. When she came back with towels to stop the bleeding, Honey was kneeling by Mimi's side. Mimi was crying, and Tasha could tell she was in pain.

"What the fuck happened to you?" Honey asked her.

"Them bitches jumped me!" Mimi yelled.

Amra looked down at Mimi, and knew it had to be a group of girls for Mimi to be beaten up so badly. "Damn! How many girls was it?" *Them bitches mauled her ass!*

The girls helped Mimi up and took her into her room and laid her on her bed. There was a deep cut in her side, and little cuts on her face. She had a busted lip, and she complained that her ribs were sore from being stomped.

Tasha went and got some Tylenol from the bathroom cabinet and gave them to Mimi.

After they cleaned Mimi up, she fell asleep.

Honey shook her head. "I shouldn't have let her go out by herself."

Amra was standing in the doorway with her hands on her hip. She looked at Tasha and said, "I'm going back to sleep. Let me know if y'all need me."

Tasha turned to Honey. "Me too. We'll deal with it in the morning. It ain't too much we can do tonight anyway." She turned and walked out of the room and crawled into her own bed. *I hope it don't be drama like this every night. What type of beef do she got anyway? I hope she ain't gonna be starting shit all over town, because I am not trying to be fighting every time I leave the house.* Tasha went to sleep with a lot on her mind, hoping her new experience would be what she expected it to be.

A couple weeks passed before Mimi left the house. The girls who had jumped her had messed her up pretty badly, and she didn't want to leave the house looking tore up. Her wounds healed quickly, but one of the scratches on her face left a small scar above her eyebrow. Mimi was furious. In all her years of fighting, she had never been hit in the face, and she was determined to get back at the chicks that had done it. "I am beating them bitches down when I see them," she exclaimed as she sat at the table and ate breakfast.

No one commented. Mimi had been talking about getting even with the girls ever since the day after the fight.

"I heard they gon' be at the party tonight," Mimi said, referring to a party that was going down at a local club.

Honey quickly replied, "Well, that's where we gonna be then."

That night, the girls headed to the party. It was Tasha's and Amra's first time getting out, and they were excited to see what life in Flint was like. When they entered the party, they immediately felt the steam emanating from the hot bodies that filled the room.

"Damn, it's packed in here!" Amra shouted over the loud music blaring from the speakers.

As the girls walked through the party, Mimi scanned for the girls who'd jumped her. "They're not here," she said.

The girls found a table and sat down and enjoyed the atmosphere of the club. It was crowded, and everybody seemed to be having a good time.

Tasha looked out onto the dance floor and saw people grinding against each other. She sat back and chilled with her girls, enjoying herself. The clubs in Flint were different from the ones back home. They were wilder, and Tasha liked the change.

Amra got up and went out onto the dance floor, pulling Tasha along with her. The girls started to dance, and men instantly jumped at the chance to be close to them.

A dude began dancing with Tasha from behind. She turned around and saw that he was butt-ass ugly. *Hell nah, brother!* she thought and slyly danced away from him.

Amra started to laugh, and Tasha made her way off the floor. Amra danced with a group of dudes and left the dance floor with one of them, and headed to the bar. She flirted coyly with the dude, and when she ran out of conversation, they exchanged numbers, and she rejoined her friends at their table.

The party lasted until two o'clock, and when it was over, the girls were tired and ready to go home. As they were leaving the club, a tall, good-looking man called Mimi's name.

She turned her head to see who it was, and a smile slowly crept across her face. "Manolo!" she said excitedly. She left her friends and walked over to him and gave him a hug.

"What up, Mimi?" Manolo looked her up and down. "I ain't seen your ass in a while."

"You the one who be acting like a stranger," Mimi told him.

Manolo pulled out a piece of paper and wrote down his number. He handed it to her. "I got to talk to you and your girls about something. Holla at me when you get a chance."

"What's up? You might as well holla at us now."

Mimi was about to motion for her girls to come over, but Manolo stopped her. "Nah, it's about making some money. I'd rather discuss business in private. Just holla at me, ma." Manolo walked away.

Mimi walked back over to her friends.

"Who was that?" Honey asked.

"That's my boy, Manolo. We were cool back in the day. I haven't seen him in a while though. He said he want to talk to us about making some money."

Honey's eyes glistened when she heard the word *money*. She was always down for making money. "We need to get at him then."

Mimi told her friends about Manolo on their way back to the house. They all wanted to make some money, and they decided they would call him the next day to see what he was talking about.

Chapter Seven

Manolo sat down across from the group of girls and looked them all up and down as he took in their features. He passed a blunt to Mimi. "What up, Mimi baby? What the fuck you been up to?"

Mimi licked her lips, almost tasting the weed. "Shit, just chilling. What up, though? You said you wanted to holla at me and my girls. We here, so what you want?" She took a pull from the blunt then passed it to Honey, who was sitting next to her.

Manolo sat back on his black leather couch. "I got a business proposition for you and your girls. It's easy money."

"You know I'm all about making money." Mimi crossed her legs. "What you got in mind?" Manolo cleared his throat. "I saw you and your girls at the club last night. Y'all would be perfect for the job."

Tasha was listening closely to the conversation, but she was getting fed up, because Manolo was talking in circles. *I'm all down for making money, but he ain't telling me shit. He got to come with some more details.* She was up on her game and had heard how grimy Flint niggas could be. She didn't know Manolo, and wasn't sure what he wanted them for. "What exactly is it that we got to do?" she asked, not hiding her skepticism.

Manolo smiled. "A'ight, li'l mama, calm down. Look, this is what I'm saying. It's these niggas from the North Side. These niggas getting money. I know, the streets is talking. They're sitting on chips and waiting to get robbed. Your girl right here got one of they numbers last night." He pointed to Amra. "That's one of the reasons why I picked y'all, 'cause it's already an interest on they part. Now the hustle that I'm trying to do gon' take about three hours, tops. Now this gon' pop off with or without y'all, but if you down, then you and your girls gon' get in good with these niggas. The only thing y'all got to do is get them in the hotel room, and I'll do the rest."

Tasha put her hands up, rejecting the blunt that was being passed around the room. "Hold on, let me get this right. You want us to set niggas up for you to rob 'em?"

Manolo looked straight into her eyes and said, "*Exactly*!"

Honey hit the blunt, held it down for a minute, and then blew it out. "Well, shit, what do we get out of all this?"

Manolo laughed. "At the end of the night, we will come together, put the money down, and split it up. I'll give y'all fifty percent of whatever I get. Y'all can keep the jewelry and split the cash however you want."

Tasha folded her arms. "Hell nah! We're taking all the risks. I'm sure you gon' be all ski-masked up and shit. We have to worry about these dudes coming back at us."

Manolo shook his head lightly. "Ma, don't even worry about that. The way I'm gon' do it, they gon' think y'all getting robbed with them. See, what I was thinking, y'all could lure these cats into a hotel room. Make them think they 'bout to get in on some freaky ménage-à-troistype shit, and that's when I come into the picture—handcuffs and everything. I'll catch them in a vulnerable situation."

"Since we taking all the risks, we want seventy-five/twenty-five," Honey stated firmly. "Fifty percent between four people ain't a lot."

Manolo hadn't expected them to bargain with him, but he was money-hungry, and these cats had too much dough to let the opportunity pass. "Deal! Now, is y'all down or what?"

Honey looked at Mimi and shrugged her shoulders, not knowing whether or not she should give the proposition any thought.

"You know I don't give a fuck." Mimi grabbed the blunt from Honey. "Let's get those niggas."

Honey looked at Amra and could see she was unsure about the situation.

"What do you think, Tasha?" Amra asked.

Tasha thought about it for a minute, then did the math in her head. "It's cool. I'm down. I'm not about to pass up no scratch."

Amra sighed, figuring that if Tasha agreed to it, then it must be all right. "I'm in."

Honey said, "So, how we supposed to hook up with them?"

Manolo nodded his head at Amra. "It's a party tonight. They gon' be there, and since Amra already got one of them interested in her, then she can just introduce the rest of y'all when you get there."

Honey said, "Okay, but it takes money to get ready for a party like this, and since we ain't making money yet—"

"If you can hustle them niggas like you hustling me, then we straight." Manolo laughed. He knew that the dark-skinned beauty sitting in front of him was a hustler at heart. It was obvious that she was the leader of the crew. He reached into his pocket and counted out two thousand dollars and handed five hundred to each girl. "Y'all straight now?"

Mimi nodded. "We good."

Manolo walked out of the room, and a couple minutes later, he came back with four cell phones. "This is what you handle business on. If you ain't hustling a nigga, then he shouldn't be calling on this phone. I'll be calling too, so always keep it on." He handed a phone to each girl.

Tasha looked around his plush apartment. He had black leather furniture on top of white carpeting, and a plasma TV. *He's living kind of nice, so I guess he got money.* She saw that her friends were getting ready to leave, so she rose up and walked to the door.

The girls left the house and walked a couple blocks before hopping on the city bus. "So, what y'all think?" Mimi asked as they all piled in.

"He cool, and I'm definitely down to do this shit," Amra replied.

Honey laughed. "Hell yeah, we down to do this shit. First, we about to go get some outfits for tonight, though."

The girls headed to the Valley, Flint's only shopping center, and immediately split up. Tasha hit store after store trying to find an outfit that she could afford. Eventually, she bought a black dress that was completely out in the back. It wrapped around her neck and barely covered her breasts, and the bottom clung tightly to her voluptuous hips. She tried it on, put her hands on her hips and looked into the mirror. *Hell yeah, this dress is nice.* She looked at her flat stomach, then turned around and looked at her butt to see if it looked too big. She looked at Honey and asked her, "What about this?"

Honey looked at the outfit and immediately nodded in approval.

Tasha smiled then looked at the price tag. "Damn! Four hundred and twenty dollars!" she said aloud. "I thought this was on the clearance rack!"

"Girl, Macy's be taxing on they clothes. In a minute, you ain't gon' have to shop on the clearance rack."

Honey bought a bluejean skirt that was so short, it barely covered what it was supposed to. She bought a black one-sleeve shirt and black strapped sandals that laced up to her ankle.

They walked around the store until they found Amra and Mimi. They were trying on clothes. Amra ended up buying hip-hugging bluejean pants, a white bikini top shirt that would show her flat stomach, and a silver Gucci belt.

Mimi tried on a sleeveless black bodysuit that hugged her skin like plastic, and picked out a silver necklace to go with it. "How does this look?" she asked Tasha.

"It's cute. Buy it."

Mimi started to unzip it in the back. "Nah. I got an outfit at home that I'm gon' wear." She went into the dressing room and got dressed.

They rushed home to prepare for the party. Since they only had a couple of hours to get dressed, they started as soon as they walked through the door.

"Honey, you know you're doing my hair, right?" Amra walked into the bathroom to get the first shower.

"All right, that's cool, but hurry up, 'cuz I got to do mine too."

Tasha laughed. "Yeah, Honey, you doing my shit too."

"I'll do it if you want me too," Mimi told her.

"Yeah, it will save time," Honey stated. "She can do your makeup too."

Mimi did Tasha's hair and makeup even better than Honey could have done it, twisting Tasha's long hair into a knotted ponytail. Tasha looked in the mirror at her hair and makeup. "You about to be hooking my shit up all the time."

"You should have been letting me hook you up, instead of letting Honey mess you up!"

They laughed.

Honey walked in the room. "Bitches, I heard that!"

Mimi put on the outfit she had tried on in the store. Tasha knew for a fact that Mimi hadn't bought it, and seemed to be the only one who had noticed that. Tasha didn't say anything about it, though. She just went and got dressed.

By nine thirty, everybody was ready to go. They asked Tammy if they could borrow her car. When Tammy agreed, they jumped into the red Monte Carlo and left.

They walked into the party at eleven o'clock, and immediately all eyes were on them. Amra made her way through the crowd, her friends following behind. They chilled by the bar, accepting drinks from men who were trying to take them home. The music at the party was loud, and the DJ was spinning Jay-Z. The atmosphere in the club was cool, and most people were dancing in the middle of the floor, but the people who thought they were too cool to dance were sitting at the many tables that surrounded the room. It was dark, with the exception of a strobe light and the light coming from the bar, so it was hard for Amra to spot the guy she had talked to the night before at the club.

Mimi leaned over and asked Amra. "Do you see him?"

Amra shrugged her shoulders. "It's too dark. I can't really see anybody."

Honey jumped up off the stool she was seated on and said, "Come on, we can't find them. Fuck it! We'll just have to tell Manolo they didn't come. I didn't buy this outfit just to sit around. I'm about to go dance." She disappeared into the crowd. As soon as she entered the crowd, she drew new attention as she danced in the middle of the floor.

Amra looked around, and gave up when she was sure that she couldn't find him in the dark. She looked at Mimi and Tasha and shrugged her shoulders.

"Don't trip," Tasha said. "We can do it another night."

Amra ordered a drink from the bar.

"What up?"

She turned around when she heard the deep voice, and saw a dark-skinned dude with corn-rows standing close behind her.

"What up?" she replied, not trying to show her interest in him.

The man stood close to her as he bent down to whisper in her ear, "It looks like you waiting on somebody. I don't wanna throw salt on your game, so I'm gonna cut to the chase. Can I get your number so I can call you later?"

Amra wanted to deny him, but his intriguing smile and dark skin tone lured her in. She was about to reply when Honey came back out of the crowd smiling, and stepped directly in between Amra and the dude she was talking to. Honey looked at him rudely and said, "Excuse me!" and he took a step back. She turned to Amra. "Fuck them niggas! It's these dudes sitting over there. I just danced with one of 'em. Let's go chill with them."

Amra nodded her head okay, and Honey began to walk away. Before leaving the bar, Amra wrote down her number and handed it to him. "What did you say your name was?" she asked him.

He rubbed his neatly trimmed goatee. "Lloyd."

Honey led the way over to her new friends, and Amra immediately spotted the dude from the night before. "That's him!" she whispered excitedly in Honey's ear.

Honey's smile immediately got ten times brighter as she took a seat next to the guy she'd been dancing with. The girls sat down in between the group of dudes.

Amra sat down next to the guy she had talked to and said, "What up?"

The dude was as high as a kite. He looked at her and his eyes lingered on her breasts, which were easily visible from the bikini top she had on. "What up, ma? What did you say your name was last night?"

Amra couldn't be too upset at him for forgetting her name, because she didn't remember his either. "Amra," she said.

"Seneca." He hit the blunt he was smoking and passed it to her.

Amra relaxed as she let the weed fill her lungs. Seneca was all over her, but she didn't seem to mind. She was dancing in front of him as he put his hands on her body, touching every place that she would let him go. She noticed the platinum necklace that hung low from his neck, the diamonds glistening brightly. *Yeah, he got money,* she thought to herself as she drank the Hennessy she had bought from the bar. She looked around and noticed that her friends were having a good time too. Seneca's friends were all over Mimi, Tasha, and Honey.

The party started to wind down, and they all walked out to the parking lot.

Seneca looked at Amra and said, "Roll out with me tonight."

Hell yeah! I'm about to get this nigga! Amra looked at him and his boys, and then said, "Well,

it's still early. Y'all want to come back to our hotel room?"

Seneca was the first to speak up. "Yeah, that
sound good." He looked at his boys and asked,
"Y'all trying to roll?"

They all quickly replied, "Hell yeah," at the
same time.

A smile spread across Amra's face. She could
hear the eagerness in the men's voices. They
thought they were getting some ass. She looked
back at her girls and winked her eye. Now the
only thing they needed was Manolo to come
through.

They instructed the group of guys to follow
their cab to the hotel. After they got into the cab,
Mimi immediately picked up her phone to call
Manolo. "It's all set up. They're meeting us at
the room you checked out for us." Manolo said
something to her, and she hung up the phone.
She looked at her friends and informed them
about what was going down. "He said that the
key will be waiting at the front desk under my
name. He wants us to get them drunk. Y'all know
the rest. He's gonna be waiting in the bathroom,
and when he hears the signal, he's gon' come and
rob they asses blind."

Tasha frowned up. "What's the signal?"

Mimi answered, "Oh yeah, when we turn out
the lights, he knows to come in."

The girls were silent for the rest of the ride.

Tasha looked at the illuminated streets of the city. *I hope we get away with this shit. It seems too easy. Manolo better be there, 'cuz I'm not trying to fuck these niggas for real.*

The cab finally arrived at the hotel, and butterflies filled their stomachs. Tasha was nervous and tried not to show it as she looked at her friends. She gave the cabby a ten-dollar bill and got out of the car.

Seneca and his carful of friends pulled up. Their music could be heard for blocks away, and announced their arrival before the car actually pulled up. Seneca stuck his head out of the window. "I'm 'bout to park in the lot. Meet us in the lobby."

Amra spread a fake smile across her face and yelled, "Okay. Is y'all trying to drink something?"

He replied, "Yeah. Do y'all got some drank already?"

Honey interjected, "Nah, but we drinking Rémy."

Seneca looked at Honey and replied, "A'ight, I hear you, ma. We'll buy. I'ma hit the corner store. We'll be back in ten minutes. What's the room number?"

Mimi quickly replied, "Two-o-four. Hurry up, so we can get the party started."

With that, Seneca and his boys pulled off, headed for the liquor store. As soon as the girls saw the taillights pull out of the parking lot, they entered the hotel and approached a woman sitting behind the front desk. She had an outrageous hairdo and big gold hoop earrings.

Mimi was the first to speak, "Hello, my name is Mimi—"

The woman pulled a key out and said, "Hurry up. Manolo is waiting for you upstairs."

Mimi took the key, and they headed to the second floor.

When the girls reached the room, Amra hesitated at the door. She was beginning to have second thoughts. "I don't know about this," she whispered to her friends as they stood outside the room.

Honey looked at Amra and smacked her lips. "Well, it's too late now. We're here and we got them niggas on their way, so you better get your shit together before they get here. And stop looking so nervous. You a dead giveaway."

Tasha was nervous too, she just hadn't said it aloud. She looked skeptically at Honey, and then at Amra. "Come on, Amra. It's easy money. It won't take that long. Let's just get it over with," she said, trying to convince herself too.

They entered the room, and Manolo came out of the bathroom with bluejeans, a white T-shirt, and a black ski mask rolled up around his face. "Is everything set up?" he asked.

Tasha could see the dollar signs in his eyes, "Yeah, they're on their way."

Manolo pulled his gun from his waistline. "Cool." He sat on the bed with the gun in his palm. "Just follow through with the plan, and we are about to get paid. What kind of car were they driving?"

Honey looked in the air, trying to remember what kind of car they had been in. "I don't know. It was one of them new boys. I think it was an Excursion . . . yeah, a silver one. It was sitting on some nice rims, though. I do remember that."

Manolo rubbed his hands together. "That's mine too. I can use some rims for the whip."

At that moment, they heard a knock at the door, and everyone immediately froze.

Oh, shit! I wonder if they heard us talking. Tasha looked around the room. She could tell that the same thought was on everybody's mind.

Manolo whispered, "Showtime!" He hurried to the bathroom and closed the door.

Amra yelled, "One minute!" and all the girls sat on the bed, trying not to look suspicious. She walked to the door and opened it.

Seneca and his friends walked in, holding brown paper bags in their hands. Seneca had a blunt in his mouth and a big smile on his face.

Tasha watched as the group of dudes entered the room. They all seemed to rush her way, but the fat, ugly one reached her first.

Honey saw the look on Tasha's face when he introduced himself, and she wanted to laugh. *Damn, that nigga look just like Biggie Smalls!* She turned around, trying to muffle her laugh.

"I'm Rico," he said cockily.

"Tasha," she replied with a sexy smile. She looked him up and down. The nigga was ugly, but she had to admit, he was geared from head to toe. *This is a fly-ass fat mu'fucka,* she thought to herself. The platinum chain with the diamond cuts in it made her warm up to him quickly.

"You drinking something?" Rico held up his bottle of Rémy.

Tasha hated the taste of liquor. "Crack it open." She went and got some plastic cups off of the sink that sat outside the bathroom door, and walked back over to him. She stood directly in between his legs as he filled her cup. She sipped on her drink as she watched him kill cup after cup of the hard liquor.

Amra walked over to the radio and turned it on to keep everyone entertained.

Seneca walked around to all his boys and tipped the bottle of Rémy that he had, so they could bless it. Each dude tapped the top of the bottle before he finally popped it open.

Tasha looked around and saw that her friends had finally begun to relax. At first the air was filled with tension, but once they got some liquor in their systems, they began to act normal.

"So, where you from?" Rico asked her.

Tasha frowned. "Where you from?"

Rico smiled slyly. "I'm from here. This is home, baby girl. I'm a North Side nigga all day."

Tasha smiled as she listened to Rico rep his 'hood. His speech was slow, and he was emphasizing every word. She knew it was only a matter of time before he got pissy drunk.

"I got to piss," Rico said abruptly. He got up to go to the bathroom.

Tasha stood up with him, her heart pounding. "Wait!" she yelled.

"I'll be right back." Rico got up and walked into the bathroom.

Tasha closed her eyes, waiting to hear something, and Amra's eyes bucked as she sat completely still. Honey looked over at Tasha, and could see the panic in her face.

Tasha walked over to the bathroom door. Just as she was about to knock, Rico walked out of the bathroom and saw Tasha waiting for him. *That was close!* she thought to herself.

She entered the bathroom and locked the door once she was inside. The bathroom was empty. She was relieved, because she thought for sure that they would be caught. She looked into the tiny mirror and saw Manolo step from behind the shower curtain. He had reacted quickly and jumped behind the curtain when Rico had come in.

She turned around, and he walked close up on her and pressed his dick against her ass cheeks. Tasha could feel his body heat, and her breathing got deeper and deeper. Manolo leaned over and whispered in her ear, "Go back out there and get this shit started."

Tasha just nodded her head and walked out the door, nervous about the possibility of the dudes peeping their game. She made eye contact with Mimi, who then looked over to Honey.

Amra already had Seneca tipsy. She was sitting on his lap, facing him, and his hands were on her ass.

Tasha walked over to the bed where Rico had laid down and kicked his feet up.

"Come here." He rubbed the bed beside him. "You look kind of uncomfortable."

Tasha wanted to gag. She walked over to the dresser and filled her cup with Alizé. "You want some?" she asked him.

"Yeah, bring that shit over here."

Tasha walked over to Rico and straddled him, and his hands quickly moved to her backside. "Here." She gave him the cup full of Alizé, and he quickly downed the drink and focused his attention back on her. "I'm feeling it," she lied. She hadn't even drunk that much. In fact, she'd been sipping on the same cup all night.

"Me too." Rico began to rub his hands all over her body.

Tasha kissed him and pressed her body firmly against his. She looked back at her girls, who were all doing their own thing. She made eye contact with Honey, and Honey winked her. Then she stood up and said, "I'm feeling freaky." She'd said it loud enough for all of Seneca's boys to hear.

The dude she'd been paired up with said, "Shit! Well, come back over here."

Honey walked over to Tasha and lay in the bed with her and Rico. She whispered in his ear, "I'm really freaky." She reached over and grabbed the back of Tasha's head and kissed her on the mouth, and Tasha kissed her back.

Rico's dick got harder and harder. The sight of the two gorgeous women beside him had him horny as hell.

Tasha got up and walked over to the dude Honey had been with. She quickly got on top of his lap and said, "Let me tie you up."

The dude didn't think twice. "Damn, ma! You get down like that?" He lay back on the bed.

Tasha began to take off her clothes. She stripped all the way down to her bra and panties, and then made her way over to the drawer and pulled out some extra sheets. She tore the sheets and tied his arms to the top of the bedposts. She then tied his feet down and climbed on top of him. She looked around the room and saw that her friends were following her lead. She unbuttoned the button-up shirt he was wearing, and began to take off his pants. She kissed his stomach and made her way down to his boxers. She pulled them down to his ankles, exposing his hard dick. She had to admit, the nigga was well hung.

"Hey, ma, turn out the lights, and then suck something."

Tasha looked at her girls to make sure they were ready. Honey had Rico tied down to the bed, and Mimi and Amra had their dudes tied to the chairs that sat behind the wooden desks.

The dude that was tied to the bed watched Tasha's ass shake with each step as she walked over to the wall to the switch. He saw her caramel skin and thick shape, and couldn't wait to fuck her. "Damn! Come on, girl!"

Tasha turned around and smiled, then flicked the light switch.

Manolo walked out of the bathroom and yelled, "Stupid mu'fuckas! I want all your money and your shine!" He walked over to the switch and turned on the lights.

"What the fuck?" Seneca said as he looked at Manolo.

Manolo was pointing the gun directly in his face. He yelled at the girls, "Check all they pockets!"

Tasha looked at Honey in confusion. *They aren't supposed to know we had anything to do with this!* She walked over to Rico and picked up his clothes that were lying on the floor. She quickly went through his pockets and cleared them of all the cash she could find.

"Take his shine too!" Manolo yelled loudly.

Rico looked in Tasha's eyes as she reached around his neck to take his platinum chain. She was close enough for him to whisper in her ear, "I'm gon' find you, dirty-ass bitch!"

Tasha's breath stuck in her throat. She took his money and his chain and put them in the bag Manolo was holding.

"Put y'all's clothes back on," he said.

The girls, all scared and nervous, fumbled with their clothes. This wasn't going down the way they had expected it to. When they finally got dressed, Manolo instructed Tasha to get Seneca's car keys. She grabbed the keys, and Manolo and the girls walked out of the front door.

"Get in their ride and follow me." Manolo could see the fear in Tasha's eyes.

She got in Seneca's truck, and the rest of them hopped in Manolo's car. Her heart was beating hard as she followed him to a warehouse and pulled the truck inside. She hopped out and quickly jumped into Manolo's car. They then made their way to Manolo's house, where he dumped the money on his living room table as soon as they got inside.

"Damn!" Mimi said as she saw the bills spill out of the bag.

"I thought they weren't gonna know we had anything to do with it!" Tasha yelled. "What if these niggas come after us?"

Manolo calmly said, "They won't. It's a million bitches in this city. You won't run into them niggas again." He sat down and started counting the money.

Tasha calmed down and sat beside him as she watched.

Honey grabbed all the jewelry from the table and put it in the bag that Manolo had put the money in. "We'll pawn this shit first thing tomorrow," she said.

Manolo finished counting the money, and then announced, "Seventeen thousand five hundred."

Honey laughed. "Damn!"

Manolo handed her $8,750, and she then divided it equally between her friends. Each girl left his house with a little over $2,000.

When they got back to the house, Tasha walked into her bedroom and lay in her bed. She looked at her old cell phone and checked her messages. There were no messages in her phone. She had hoped that Joe might have called her, but it was apparent that he had either forgotten about her, or wanted to forget about her. She wished he'd told her how he felt about her. One of the main reasons why she'd left New York was because she thought she didn't have anyone there. *He didn't act like he wanted to be with me. Fuck him!*

Tasha put her old phone in an old shoebox and tossed it under her bed. She sat back on her bed, and visions of what had just happened popped into her head. All she could think about

was the look on the guys' faces when Manolo
busted out of the bathroom. She remembered
how the particular guy she was talking to didn't
even take his eyes off of her as they were being
robbed. She heard Rico's threats play in her head
over and over again, and hoped she'd never run
into him on the street. She lay down in her bed
and fell asleep.

By the time Tasha woke up the next morning,
all of her friends were already up and dressed.
They were excited, talking about what had happened the night before at the hotel.

Amra walked into the room and sat down at
the end of Tasha's bed. "It's about time you woke
up. We were just talking about last night. That
shit was crazy! It was easy money."

Tasha was still a little skeptical about what
they'd done, but the money made her feel better
about it. "Hell yeah! Two grand ain't bad for a
couple hours work."

Amra nodded. "Come on, get up. Tammy got
some food down there," she said, and left the
room.

Tasha got out of bed and walked downstairs
and into the kitchen. She smelled the aroma of
eggs, bacon, and pancakes, and immediately

grabbed a plate. "Hey, Tammy." Tasha opened the refrigerator and poured herself some orange juice.

"Morning, baby girl," Tammy greeted back.

Tasha sat down at the table next to Honey and ate her food.

Just as Amra was about to sit down next to Mimi, her cell phone rang. She put down her plate and picked it up. "Hello?"

"What up, ma?"

Amra frowned up, not recognizing the deep, melodic voice on the other end. "Who is this?" she asked.

"Lloyd."

Amra smiled as she remembered the dude she'd met at the party the night before. With all the action that had happened last night, he'd slipped her mind. She was glad he'd called though. He was fine, and she liked his style. He hadn't approached her with lame lines like so many other men did.

"What do you have planned for today?" he asked her.

"Nothing. Why? What's up with you?" She was hoping he would say he wanted to see her.

Mimi laughed and whispered, "Damn! Amra's blushing and shit."

Honey and Tasha laughed loudly.

Amra put the cell phone to her chest. "Shh!" Then she put the phone back up to her ear. "Where you at?"

"I'm at the crib, but I'm trying to come see you."

Amra smiled. "Trying to, or going to?"

Lloyd laughed. "Where you stay? I'll pick you up."

"Hold on, okay?" Amra put the phone to her chest then looked at her friends. "He wants to come pick me up. What do I say?"

Mimi frowned. "Say yeah, bitch!"

Honey hit Mimi on the arm and quickly said, "No! Say no! Nobody should know where we stay at. Shit, we don't know who knows who in Flint. We don't want none of them niggas from last night to find us. He doesn't need to know where you live."

Amra nodded her head. "I'll meet you. Where you trying to eat at?"

Lloyd told Amra to just come to his house.

An hour later, Mimi dropped Amra off at Lloyd's house, an average-looking two-story brownstone. The inside wasn't too spectacular either. Amra just figured that he spent his money on other things.

"How long I got you for?" He asked her as he sat next to her on his couch.

Amra shrugged her shoulders. "How long you wanna have me for?"

Lloyd licked his lips then kissed her. She didn't resist either. She was just as ready as he was to get shit popping. She didn't want him to think she was a ho though, so she pulled away from him.

"Don't trip. We can just chill."

Amra nodded. She said, "Let's do something." She wanted to get out of his house as soon as possible. She knew that she would eventually give up the ass if there was a bed or a couch around. *Hell, I'll fuck him on the floor!* she thought as he walked her out of the door.

They got into a black Ford Navigator. The inside of his truck was right. He had TV's in his headrests, and a DVD in his glove compartment.

"Let's go shopping," Lloyd said.

That's what the fuck I'm talking about! Buy me some shit!

Lloyd pulled up to the mall, and they got out and went into the store. Amra was geeked. *This nigga 'bout to buy me some shit, and this is my first time chilling with him.*

Lloyd walked through the mall with Amra walking proudly by his side. They went into almost every store and bought clothes, shoes, and jewelry. "You hungry?" he asked her as they passed the food court.

Amra smiled. "Yeah."

By the time they left the mall, their hands were filled with bags. Unfortunately for Amra, none of the bags belonged to her. *I can't believe he had me walking around the mall for six hours, and the only thing he bought me was some food!* She was salty, but she didn't let him know that.

They went back to his house. They talked and got to know each other a little better. It was late, and Amra was ready to go home, but she didn't want Lloyd to know where she lived. "Can I use your bathroom?" she asked.

Lloyd pointed toward it, and she got up and walked down the hall. She picked up her phone and dialed Mimi's number. Mimi didn't answer, so she tried Tasha. When Tasha didn't answer, she hung up. *It ain't even no use in calling Honey. They are probably all together anyway.* She walked back out and sat next to Lloyd.

They stayed up until three in the morning, talking to each other, and she was glad she'd stayed.

When Lloyd led Amra into his bedroom, she asked him sweetly, "Do you have something I can sleep in?"

Lloyd threw her a white T-shirt, and watched Amra take off her clothes. He saw her skinny body and her big breasts and grabbed her from behind.

Amra got in the bed with him and got close to him. She felt that he wanted her, but she was still upset that he hadn't bought her anything from the mall. *No ass for you,* she thought as she pressed her body against his as hard as she could, teasing him, trying to show him what he was missing. She turned around, and he put his arm around her, and they both went to sleep.

The ringing of her cell phone woke her up the next day. "Yeah?" she answered sleepily.

A concerned Tasha was on the phone, "You all right?"

"Yeah, I'm cool. Come pick me up."

Amra quietly got out of Lloyd's bed, put on her jeans, kept on his shirt, grabbed her purse, and walked out of the house. She waited outside for her friends. They finally pulled up, and she got into the car.

"What happened?" Mimi asked.

"Nothing, really. We just chilled."

Honey laughed in disbelief. "Okay, just chilled."

Amra was too tired to argue with her friends. She shook her head. "Okay, I'm trying to tell y'all hoes that nothing happened. We were just chilling. We went to the mall, got something to eat, and we talked the whole night."

Honey shook her head. "So, where yo' bags at?"

"He didn't buy me anything."

Mimi yelled, *"What?"*

Tasha laughed. "Dang! They just met. Y'all know a nigga ain't about to come out his pockets for a chick he just met."

"So you didn't fuck him?" Mimi asked.

"No."

Honey said, "As fine as he is, I would have."

They all laughed as they headed back to the house.

Lloyd woke up to an empty bed. He searched his house, expecting Amra to be there. *She cool,* he thought to himself. He was feeling her because she didn't trip when he didn't buy her anything at the mall. *I ain't looking for a money-hungry bitch.* He went into his bathroom and ran a shower. He liked that she didn't let him fuck her on the first night. Not many chicks would've done that.

He came back into the bedroom and saw her shirt lying on the floor. *I'll call her and tell her I'll bring it to her,* he thought. That would be a good excuse to see her again.

Amra smiled to herself, thinking about how much money she was about to get out of Lloyd. She knew he had it. She just had to get close to him. She had already decided that she was gonna fuck him, and felt he may as well pay for it. She went into her room and closed the door. *I hope he calls me,* she thought to herself. If he called her first, then he was really interested. If she had to call him, that meant he wasn't really feeling her.

She lay down in her bed and thought about what she would buy with the money she got from Lloyd. "I got to get it first," she said aloud. She turned off her cell phone, put the covers over her head, and went to sleep thinking about Lloyd and the money that was to be made. *I still can't believe he didn't buy me anything at the mall yesterday, ol' stingy-ass nigga. I bet you when he get a shot of this pussy he gon' be coming out his pockets!*

Chapter Eight

Once Manolo caught wind of Amra's new boy-friend, he quickly convinced her to juice Lloyd for money too. Manolo didn't care what the girls did, as long as they helped him make money. He knew how to manipulate people and get them to do exactly what he wanted. He taught Amra how to hit Lloyd's pockets slowly, guaranteeing her it would only take three months for her to do it, and told her that this type of lick paid even more, because it was continuous. He told her to get into Lloyd's head, and his pockets would soon follow.

Amra followed his instructions carefully, and just as Manolo predicted, Lloyd was quickly giving Amra thousands of dollars at a time.

The other girls quickly adapted to this hustle, because it wasn't as dangerous as setting groups of men up to get robbed. It wasn't hard for the girls to get money out of men, so it was even easier for Manolo to convince them to do it.

Manolo promised to put them up on some of the most 'hood-rich niggas in Flint, if they stayed on his team. The only thing he asked for was a small finder's fee. "I can have you associating in circles that you couldn't get into on your own. I know a lot of people."

There was no denying that Manolo's shit was tight. He knew where to be, who was gon' be there, and what they were worth. No matter how private a party was supposed to be, Manolo knew somebody who knew somebody that could get them in.

Once the foundation of their hustle was laid, it was easy for Tasha, Mimi, Amra, and Honey to get anything they wanted from any man.

Amra had quickly hustled $7,000 from Lloyd, and the rest of the girls quickly followed suit.

All four girls sat on the floor in the room. "Hell yeah!" Mimi exclaimed as she counted out the $6,500 that she got from some dude.

Honey pulled out a wad of money and said, "Six gees!"

Tasha laughed and threw twenty-dollar bills in the air. "Eighty-five hundred, beating all y'all hoes!"

They gave each other high fives and looked at all the money that lay scattered in the middle of the floor. Between the four of them, they had hustled $28,000. It was easier than they had expected. The three months had basically flown by, and after the first month of a dry spell, the money just poured in.

Mimi pulled out a bottle of Hennessy from underneath her bed. "Fuck me, pay me!"

"Save that shit for later, Mimi. We got to go see Manolo." Honey pulled out her cell phone. She put her finger to her mouth and motioned for her girls to be quiet as she called him.

The phone rang twice before Manolo answered his cell, "Yo'?" He answered coolly, not knowing who was on the other line.

"Manolo, this is Honey. I got something for you," she said in a teasing way, trying to make him think she was talking about more than money.

"Come through then," he said.

Honey smiled and hung up her phone. "Let's go." She hopped up off the floor with the money that she had made in her hand.

The girls quickly grabbed their money off the floor and followed Honey out to Tammy's car.

Manolo rubbed his chin. "So what you got for me?"

The girls pulled the money out of their purses and placed it on the table that separated them from Manolo.

Manolo eyes lit up. He didn't expect them to get this much money on their first hustle. He looked at Honey's cocoa-colored skin and model-type appearance, Tasha's curvy, but perfectly proportioned shape and hazel eyes, Amra's skinny figure and big breasts, and Mimi's fat ass and full lips. *Shit! A man would have to be a fool not to fall for any one of them.* He looked at Honey, and wondered what it would be like to have sex with her.

He grabbed the money from the table and started counting it. It didn't take him long, because he was an expert when it came to counting money. "Twenty-eight thousand." He took $2,800 off the top and handed each girl $6,300. He didn't mind that his share was smaller, because they would get better and better. *The more money they make, the more money I make.*

Mimi liked the feel of six thousand in her pocket, and wanted to make more. "You got another clique for us to get at?"

Manolo shook his head. "Nah, ma. We gon' hit a 'hood then switch it up. That way, y'all won't get hot. Niggas won't know y'all coming. I'll have more information in a couple days, so just keep your phones on. I'll be calling."

The girls waited anxiously for Manolo's call. They liked hustling dudes for their money. It was

like a cat-and-mouse game, and they were per-
fecting it with every clique they went through.
Each girl had her own unique style, her own way
of getting her way with a man.

Honey was smart, and it was easy for her to
get inside the heads of the men that she hustled.
She made them feel like they were the only one
for her, and she stroked their ego by calling them
Daddy, and doing anything they asked of her.
It didn't matter to her what. She did whatever
she thought would please a man. If a nigga told
her to shut up, then she stopped talking. If he
wanted her to cook him food, she made him the
best meal he'd ever tasted. If he asked her to
wash his nasty-ass drawers, she hand-washed
them to make sure that they smelled as good as
they possibly could before he put them on his ass
again. She never complained and never got into
his business. She didn't even question him about
other chicks or pester him about when he was
going to spend time with her. She simply made
herself available whenever he wanted to see her,
and made him think he was the only one she was
making herself available for. She knew that by
the end of the three months, he would pay for
everything she had done for him.

Even though Honey did whatever they asked
of her, she was always in control. "A good wom-

an always makes the man think that your ideas are his ideas," she always told Amra whenever they talked about the game.

But Amra had her own way of hustling dudes, and it paid off hansomely. She used sex to her advantage. She didn't care what she did. If she thought it would get her money, she was all for it. She would meet her target "by chance" in the club, or on the street, and that night, she would be in his bed. When they wanted their dick sucked, she sucked it. If they wanted to run trains, she let them. "Fuck me, pay me!" had quickly become her motto as well. Amra knew her pussy was good. Once men got a taste of it, they always begged for more, so it was easy for her to ask them for whatever she wanted.

She knew they would give it to her just to keep fucking her.

Amra wanted endless money, though, so she picked up the habit of hustling different niggas at the same time, blatantly ignoring Manolo's rule to not hustle more than one dude from the same 'hood. As long as they had the paper, she was insistent on taking it from whatever dude was dumb enough to fall for her game. She would suck or fuck anybody for the right price. "I don't give a fuck who he is or where he's from," she would tell Mimi whenever she tried to warn her about breaking the rule.

Mimi, on the other hand, was like the chick from the 'hood. She had grown up in the middle of the Fifth Ward, so she could relate to anyone from the streets. Niggas liked to keep her around because she already knew her role. She was hip to the streets, so she was easy to tame . . . or so she made them think. Mimi used her sexuality to satisfy her marks too, and was willing to do any and everything to get the job done. She made niggas trust her, and it wasn't long before they had her cooking the coke and bagging the weed.

Mimi became the down-ass bitch to any thug Manolo referred her to. She always made sure she made extra money, though. Since the thugs she dealt with almost always trusted her with whatever supply they were dealing, she always put a little bit in the baggy and a little bit in her purse. When Tasha tried to stop her from taking shit from the dudes she conned, she would say, "A hundred or two extra dollars a week wasn't bad for drugs that I got for free in the first place."

Tasha's method was different from all of her girls. She thought highly of herself, and simply gave niggas the pleasure of having her on their arms. She made niggas feel honored to be in her presence, and made sure to establish a friendship before she talked about being their woman. Tasha never asked for money, and when they offered it to her, she always said no. She knew what she was doing though, because the next time she checked her purse or coat, there would always be hundreds, sometimes thousands of dollars inside. She caught men by their hearts, not by their dicks, which was one reason her hustle worked so well.

Tasha never had sex with anyone she was trying to hustle, because she looked at each situation as a job. Since she wasn't a prostitute, she didn't feel that fucking men was necessary. There were other ways to get money out of them. She was simply "arm candy" and good company, nothing more.

Tasha didn't act like a ho from the block, so niggas didn't treat her like one. She was always showered with fur coats, diamond bracelets, earrings, and clothes. Since she was getting this stuff from the men she conned, she figured she didn't have to spend her money on material shit that didn't matter.

Tasha knew that eventually the money would stop coming, so she kept a shoebox underneath her bed with all of her savings. She had a hustle plan: save enough money so she could go to one of the colleges in Michigan. "Hopefully, Michigan State," she'd tell her friends when they laughed at her attempts to save money.

Tasha walked into the bathroom and saw Amra standing in the mirror. "Are you okay?" she asked Amra, noticing that her friend looked frail and worn down.

"Yeah, I'm cool. I think I'm catching the flu though. My throat hurts like hell, and I feel weak."

"It's flu season, and that shit has been going around like crazy. Well, let me get away from you before I catch it." Tasha walked out of the bathroom and yelled, "Let me know when you are done in there!"

Tasha thought about the late nights Amra had been keeping lately. *I hope she ain't taking this hustling shit too far. She is starting to look burnt out, like she's doing too much. She's trying to hustle four and five different niggas at a time. That shit is going to catch up with her. Manolo's putting her on to more capers than any of us. I hope he ain't trying to turn her out. That nigga been trying to play his hand at being a pimp. I hope she ain't getting into no dumb shit by fucking with him.*

Tasha was engrossed in her thoughts when Honey walked into the room. "Tasha, someone's on the phone for you," she said.

Tasha frowned. She hadn't given anyone Tammy's number. "Who is it?" she asked.

Honey shrugged her shoulders and threw Tasha the cordless phone. "I don't know, but it sounds important."

Tasha caught the phone and put it to her ear. "Hello?" she said, wondering who was on the other line.

"Hi. This is Dr. Danson from Grace Sinai Hospital in New York. We found your number in the purse of Patricia Rodgers. I assume this is her daughter."

"The hospital? Is she all right?"

The doctor remained calm. "I can't release information to anyone but family. Is this a family member that I am speaking with?"

"Yes, I'm her daughter. Is she okay?"

The doctor was silent for a minute.

"Hello?"

"Ms. Rodgers is in intensive care. She collapsed at her workplace. We found a cancerous tumor that needs to be tended to. She is conscious, but this needs to be taken care of before the cancer spreads. Is there any way you can come to the hospital?"

Tasha felt like she'd been smacked. She just stood there gripping the phone. *Cancer? How could Ms. Pat have cancer?* She walked over to her dresser, and with shaky hands grabbed a pen and paper. She was in such a rush that she knocked some pictures off the top.

Amra came prancing into the room and immediately saw Tasha's worried look.

"Yes. My sister and I will be there as soon as we can. Please take care of her." Tasha hung up the phone and looked at Amra.

Amra could see that something was wrong. "What's up?"

"It's your mom. She's in the hospital. They think that she has cancer."

Amra looked at Tasha, not wanting to believe what she had told her. She hadn't spoken to her mother since they'd left New York a year ago. "We have to go home," she said as tears started to flow down her face.

Tasha walked over to Amra and hugged her tightly. "Everything is going to be okay," Tasha said, but inside her heart, she knew cancer was deadly, and she prayed that Ms. Pat would be okay.

Chapter Nine

Two days later, Tasha and Amra were on a flight back to New York. Honey and Mimi didn't come along. They wanted to stay in the Midwest so they could keep hustling.

As Tasha and Amra ran down the hallways of the hospital, rushing to get to Ms. Pat, Amra stated, "I hope she's all right." They approached the nurses' station that sat in the middle of the hallway.

Amra had taken her mother for granted for so long that she'd never thought about what she would do if anything ever happened to her. She silently prayed for God to keep her mother in her life, at least long enough for her to tell her all the things she should have said a long time ago. "Can you tell me what room Patricia Rodgers is in?" she asked the nurse, a sense of urgency in her voice.

The nurse, who didn't appear to be a day over twenty-five, rolled her eyes like they'd asked her to do something that wasn't in her job description.

Tasha slammed her hand on the front counter. "Patricia Rodgers! We need to see her now!" She then said to Amra, making sure she was loud enough for the nurse to hear, "This bitch must want me to fuck her up!"

The nurse typed the information into her computer. "She is in room eight-ten. Take the elevator to the second floor," she said with an attitude.

If Amra hadn't been in such a hurry, she would have told the nurse about her damn self. She and Tasha made their way to the second floor and walked into Ms. Pat's hospital room. Tasha gasped when she saw how sickly Ms. Pat looked. She had lost a tremendous amount of weight, a sight that brought tears to Tasha's eyes. She quickly brushed them away. She had to be strong for Amra.

Amra rushed to her mother's side. She was sleeping, so she didn't wake her. She just sat on the edge of her bed and held her hand. "I'm sorry, Mama. I didn't know you were sick," she whispered. She leaned close to kiss her mother's forehead.

Tasha walked closer to the bed and put her hands on Amra's shoulder for support. As hard as it was for her to see Ms. Pat in her current state, she knew it was ten times harder for Amra.

They heard the creak of the door as it opened, and a tall, big-nosed white man with a clipboard entered the room. He seemed surprised when he saw the two girls in the room.

"You must be her daughter. Tasha, right? She talks about you all the time," he stated in a matter-of-fact tone.

Guilt is the only word to describe the feeling that swept through Tasha's body. She felt like she had betrayed Amra for being so close to Ms. Pat. She said, "Well, er, I—I—I'm not."

Amra was aware that her mother loved Tasha as if she was her own, and although she was slightly jealous of the bond that they shared, she appreciated having Tasha in both of their lives. She grabbed Tasha's hand. "I'm her daughter, Amra, and this is my sister."

Tasha looked at Amra in surprise. Amra quickly told her, "You are our family."

Tasha dropped a tear and squeezed Amra's hand tightly.

"Well, we know that the tumor in her leg is cancerous. Right now, it is in one area, but cancer spreads very quickly. I would recommend that we start treatment as soon as possible. She would have to undergo a surgery to remove the tumor. If the cancer is still present after that, then she is going to need chemotherapy to treat and control the cancer."

Amra looked back at her mother, and then at the doctor. "When can we start?"

"I would like to start immediately, but this type of treatment requires some type of payment. Does she have health insurance?"

Tasha looked at Amra, who slowly shook her head.

"No, she doesn't have insurance," Amra said. "Is that going to stop you from helping her?"

"We will do everything in our power to keep her comfortable, but without insurance or some form of payment, we cannot perform any major surgeries. We can give her painkillers to take home."

Amra yelled, "Painkillers? My mother has cancer, and you are just going to give her some Tylenol and send her home? That's bullshit!"

The doctor remained calm. He understood the young woman's frustrations, but he had to abide by the hospital's policy. "If she doesn't have insurance, we cannot treat her. Now, I can give you the number of an agency to call. They might be able to help your family with the medical bills, but they have a lot of people on their list. There is a two-year waiting period."

Tasha thought to herself, *Everybody these days is about money. That's a damn shame.* She yelled, "She doesn't have two years! If the cancer goes untreated, she will die! Look at her!"

The doctor lowered his head. Before exiting the room, he said, "I'm sorry, but it's hospital policy. It's out of my hands. Hurley Hospital will treat her without a down payment. They're a state-mandated facility, so they can't turn her away. You might want to try over there."

Tasha stared at the doctor like he was crazy. Everybody knew that going into that hospital was like committing suicide. She looked back at Amra, who was sitting in a chair next to Ms. Pat's bed.

"What are we going to do?"

"I'll figure it out." Tasha pulled a chair next to Amra's and gripped her hand.

They sat by Ms. Pat's bedside and thought about how they could come up with enough money to cover her hospital bills. They both cried silent tears for the woman that they equally loved. They held onto her for dear life, and eventually they both drifted into an uncomfortable sleep.

The next morning, they were awakened by the commotion coming from the hallways of the hospital. Tasha looked up and saw that Amra's chair was empty. *She must have gone to get some food or something.* She saw Ms. Pat stir in her bed and thought the noise had awakened her too. She reached for Ms. Pat's hand. "Hey, Ms. Pat. How you feeling?"

Ms. Pat blinked twice, as if she couldn't believe her eyes. "Tasha? Baby, what are you doing here?" she asked weakly. She sat up and hugged Tasha's neck. "I missed you so much!"

"The doctor called and told us you were sick. Amra's here too."

Just then, Amra entered the room as if she'd been waiting for an introduction. She stood by the door, not knowing what to say to her mother. She hadn't called her since she had left for Flint, and didn't know if her mother was happy to see her or not.

"Don't be standing in the doorway like you some type of stranger. Get over here and give me a hug."

Amra rushed to her mother's side, relieved that she didn't hold a grudge. She hugged her tightly.

"Why didn't you tell me you were sick when I talked to you on the phone?" Tasha asked. "We would have come home."

Ms. Pat shrugged her shoulders and stubbornly replied, "Ain't nobody sick. These doctors are just overexaggerating. I'm fine. You girls didn't have to fly all the way home just to take care of me. The Good Lord will see to it that I make it through this just fine."

"Momma, you have cancer, and we have to do something about it. Not even God can heal this. You can't just sit around denying that you are sick."

"We're going to come up with the money to pay for your surgery, I promise," Tasha added.

Ms. Pat waved her hand, as if dismissing the idea. "Child, don't go spending all your money on me. I don't need any surgeries. If the Lord says it's my time to go, then ain't no surgery going to stop it. So let it be. I'll be all right." Ms. Pat stared lovingly at Amra, and then at Tasha. "It's just good to see you two . . . my two girls. I'm happy with just that."

Tasha looked at Ms. Pat and smiled, but on the inside she was worried. *You need to have this surgery, Ms. Pat.* Tasha's mind was racing a thousand miles a minute, trying to come up with a solution to their problem. She looked around the hospital room and instantly felt a shiver go down her spine. *I hate hospitals. They are so contagious-feeling, with all these sick people here.* She felt as if the room was closing in on her. She needed to get out of the confinement of the hospital room. She stood up. "I'm going to go find the doctor." She quickly walked out of the room, desperately wanting to breathe fresh air. She walked down the hall and spotted Ms. Pat's doctor checking a patient's chart a couple doors down. "Excuse me, Doctor Danson!" she shouted, jogging to catch up to him.

Doctor Danson turned around. "Hi. Tasha, is it?"

"Yeah. Um, Ms. Pat is awake, and we were wondering when we could take her home."

The doctor flipped through his clipboard, looking for Ms. Pat's chart. "Did your family come to a decision regarding the surgery?"

"We're going to come up with the money as soon as we can. How long do you think it will be before the cancer starts to spread?"

The doctor put his pen back in his lab coat pocket. "It depends. No one really knows how fast cancer will progress. Could be weeks, maybe months. The surgery is one hundred and fifty thousand, and we can't operate until the hospital has received twenty-five percent of the payment."

Tasha's heart dropped when she heard the amount of money they had to come up with. "So, if we get twenty-five percent of it, then you will remove the tumor?"

The doctor nodded.

"We'll get it . . . soon." Tasha began to walk away, but then stopped and asked, "Oh yeah, when will she be able to go home?"

"Today. We can't really do anything else for her. I'll prescribe some pain pills to control the pain. Just get the money quickly. If anything happens before then, just bring her into the emergency."

Amra, Ms. Pat, and Tasha slowly left the hospital and took the city bus home. When they finally made it home, Ms. Pat went to her room to rest.

"It feels good to be back in New York," Amra said.

"Yeah, it does feel good to be back home. I never thought I would say this, but I miss the big city. I just wish we had come back under better circumstances."

The girls went up to their room, and saw that everything was as they had left it.

"I wish I wouldn't have been acting funny toward my moms." Amra looked at the picture of her and her mother that was on her dresser. "I never thought she would get sick. There is so much that I wish I could take back, you know?"

"Don't trip off that shit. She knows you didn't mean anything by it. You were just going through a thang. She knows you love her. Don't beat yourself up over what happened. The only thing that matters is that you are here right now."

Amra knew that Tasha was right. Her mother knew her better than anyone else in the world, but she still wished she hadn't been so petty. She asked Tasha, "Have you heard from your mother?"

The words hit Tasha like a ton of bricks. Amra saw her friend's eyes begin to water, and she immediately wanted to take back her words. Tasha hadn't talked about her mother since the day she had come to live with them, but inside, she wished she had a family of her own. Even though Ms. Pat had been great to her, she had always grown up feeling as if a big piece of her life was missing. *Amra doesn't know how good she has it.*

Tasha despised her mother. She never understood how a mother could turn her back on a child she gave birth to. Because of her mother's drug addiction, she had never learned the little things that only a mother could teach a daughter. *I never had a mother to help me get dressed on the first day of school. No one showed me how to take care of myself when I got my first period. I had to learn how to become a woman on my own, and I still don't know if I'm getting this shit right.*

Tasha never answered Amra's question, and Amra never brought it up again.

Tasha thought about her mother all day. Her thoughts were consumed with how things might have been if she had a good mother. Tears rolled down her face as she lay in her bed, and before she knew it, she had cried herself to sleep.

Chapter Ten

The next day, Amra stayed at home with her mother while Tasha went to see about her own mother. She walked the five blocks to her old house, admiring her old neighborhood as she went. She didn't know what she was going to say to her mother when she saw her. She really didn't even want to talk to her. *I just want to make sure she's okay. Just see her face and know that she's still here.*

Tasha approached her old street and could see her mom's house from the corner. *What the fuck happened?* She rushed over to the abandoned house. It was boarded up around the windows and had an orange eviction sticker posted on the front door. She walked up to the house and opened the screen door. She still had her house key, so she entered. The house reeked of garbage. *Where is she?* She stared in utter disbelief at the trash.

She walked into her mother's old room and saw needles, empty beer bottles, trash, and used condoms all over the floor. Tasha's eyes started to water, and she felt a sense of abandonment. She wanted to ask her mother, "Why do you have to be like this?" Instead, she wiped the tears from her eyes and said, "If it's fuck me, then fuck you too!"

She pulled the key off her key ring, threw it on the floor with the rest of the trash, and walked out of the house. Tasha couldn't believe that her mother had just up and left.

She started the long walk back to Ms. Pat's house. Her emotions were crazy. She was worried and scared for Ms. Pat, and upset and in need for her own mother. She felt like an orphan, abandoned and alone.

Her cell phone rang, giving her a break from the crude reality she'd just faced. "Hello?"

"Hey, Tasha," Honey said. "How is Amra's moms doing?"

"Not so good. She has cancer. She doesn't have insurance, so the hospital won't remove her tumor. Me and Amra have to come up with almost forty thousand, I mean quick, before the shit spreads."

Honey knew how much Ms. Pat meant to Tasha, and that Amra would go nuts. "I'm so sorry,

Tash. I had no clue she was that sick. Why don't you ask Manolo for the money? You know he'll let y'all borrow it."

Tasha knew that Honey was right. Manolo would give them the money. Of course, he would tax the hell out of them with interest, but at least they would have the cash to put up for the surgery. They could worry about the rest later. "Thanks, Honey. We'll be back tomorrow night. We just want to make sure everything is okay here first. We're just trying to make her as comfortable as possible, at least until we can come up with the money to pay for her surgery."

"Y'all take your time, and tell Ms. Pat I hope she feels better. Tasha, are you all right, though? You sound like something else is fucking with you."

Tasha didn't feel like explaining the situation about her mother. "I'm cool. Look, I'll check you later."

When Tasha arrived back at Ms. Pat's house, Ms. Pat was up and moving around.

"Hey, baby." Ms. Pat walked over to Tasha and kissed her on the forehead.

"Hey. How are you feeling?"

"I'm fine."

Ms. Pat tried to act as if nothing was wrong, but Tasha could tell she was lying. "I'm glad you're feeling okay."

Ms. Pat walked into the kitchen and opened the refrigerator door. "I didn't have a chance to do much shopping. Are you hungry?"

"Yeah, but I don't want you on your feet cooking. I'll go and get us something to eat." Tasha took Ms. Pat's hand and led her to the living room couch. She ran up the stairs and entered Amra's room. "Hey, come with me to grab something to eat. I have to talk to you about something.

Tasha grabbed Ms. Pat's car keys, and the girls headed out of the door. As she drove, she reacquainted herself with the city. "I talked to Honey about an hour ago. She thinks that we should ask Manolo for the money."

Amra's eyes grew wide with optimism. "We should! I mean, you know he got it, and as much money as we're making him, he shouldn't care about us asking for nothing."

Tasha pulled into the parking lot and parked the car. "I hope he says yes. I'm going to call him tonight and tell him we have to talk to him about something."

They got out of the car and walked into the Jamaican restaurant to get some jerk chicken. They got their food and got back into their car. As they pulled out of the parking lot, a girl driving a black Yukon pulled in front of them and hit the front end of Ms. Pat's car. Tasha hit the brakes hard. "Bitch!" She put the car in park and quickly got out to inspect the damage.

"Damn! What the fuck were you doing?" Amra asked the brown-skinned girl with red hair.

"I am so sorry. Damn!" The girl nervously paced back and forth. "He gon' kill me! This ain't even my whip."

"Yeah? Well, this ain't our car either, so I hope you got insurance." Amra folded her arms and leaned against her mother's dented car.

The girl pulled out a cell phone and dialed a number. "Baby, can you come to the chicken place on Thirty-Seventh Street? I got into an accident." The girl listened on the phone for a minute, then hung up. "He's on his way. I am so sorry."

Tasha got into Ms. Pat's car and waited for someone to come.

"Hey, you want to beat that bitch ass?" Amra asked Tasha, hoping that she would say yes.

Tasha laughed. "Nah, don't trip. Just make sure she doesn't try to pull off. That bitch driving like she the shit, trying to stunt in her whip. What she need to do is fix that bad-ass weave job she got going on. Why she trying to look good in a car that ain't even hers?"

Amra chuckled. She got out of the car and stood by the door.

Tasha sighed and leaned her seat all the way back. *Today ain't my day. Dumb bitch!*

Twenty minutes later, Tasha heard someone pull up with loud music playing. "You all right, ma?" she heard a man say.

"Hell nah!" Amra yelled. With big smile on her face, she quickly walked toward Tasha and tapped on the window to alert her. Amra didn't even say anything; she just looked smugly toward the girl who'd hit their car.

"What?" Tasha asked, confused. *Ain't this about a bitch?* she thought to herself when she finally saw Joe hugging a girl tight around the waist. Tasha's heart began to pound in her chest, and she instantly became jealous. She quickly pulled down her visor and looked in the mirror. *Fuck! He would have to catch me when I'm dressed all bummy and rocking this raggedy-ass ponytail.* She quickly pulled the hair tie out and allowed her hair to flow freely. Then she pulled out her lip-gloss and applied a shiny coat to her lips. It didn't do much to improve her appearance, but it was better than nothing. She looked at her face and saw that she looked tired too. She hadn't had much time to worry about herself since she had gotten back.

Joe was inspecting his car as Tasha got out of Ms. Pat's car, and she and Amra walked toward him. When the girl approached them, Tasha immediately frowned up. *Bitch, I ain't trying to talk to you!*

The girl said to Joe, "Baby, this is the girl I hit."

Joe looked at Tasha, and the look of shock on his face made Amra burst out in laughter. She quickly turned around and walked back to the car.

Tasha's heart was pounding. She looked Joe in the eyes. "Hi."

The girl walked over to Joe, grabbed his hand and held him tight.

Amra yelled out, "Oh, hell no!"

Joe told his friend, "Go wait in the car."

The girl mean-mugged Tasha, and then looked back at Joe.

"In the car," Joe repeated.

The girl smacked her lips and got into the car.

Joe and Tasha just stared at each other, as if neither of them could believe what they were seeing. "When did you get back?" he asked her.

"Why? You didn't expect to get put into a situation like this, huh?" Tasha grinned mischievously.

"Something like that." Joe shook his head at the irony.

Tasha looked at the girl in the car. "I see you doing okay."

Joe put his head down and smirked to himself. "That's nothing. I'm trying to see what's up with you."

Tasha felt giddy, as if this was her first time meeting Joe, but she still had a little attitude because he was with another girl. It had been almost a year since she had last seen him, and when she left New York, she didn't know where they stood. Because of the jealousy that streaked through her when she saw him holding the other girl's hand, she knew she had feelings for him.

"So, what up? Can we link up later?" Joe asked her.

"Right now really ain't a good time." Tasha folded her arms across her chest.

Joe could tell that something was wrong with her. She seemed worried and looked exhausted. "It's cool. You need anything?"

Tasha smiled. "Just a new bumper for Ms. Pat's car."

Joe pulled out some money, counted out three thousand dollars, and dropped it on the hood. "This should take care of it." He had given her way more than the bumper would cost to be replaced, but he wanted to make sure she was straight since she had way too much pride to ask him for anything.

Tasha took the money and began to walk away. She turned around and waved to Joe, knowing he would still be watching her. She got into the car, and before she pulled off, she saw the girl get out of Joe's car and start yelling at him. Tasha smiled and pulled off.

"I told you we should have beat the brakes off that bitch," Amra said as they drove back to the house.

Tasha frowned. "He ain't my man, but he was looking good, though."

By the time the girls came back with the food, it was cold. Tasha told Ms. Pat what had happened to her car, and gave her the money to get it fixed.

They sat down and ate dinner with Ms. Pat. Tasha could tell Amra was happy to be near her mother again. Amra looked tired too, and Tasha knew it was from worrying about Ms. Pat.

Tasha went up to the room she shared with Amra and lay down on her old bed. *I can't believe he's fucking with that ugly bitch,* she thought, referring to the girl she had seen Joe with. *That nigga still got it, though, with his fine ass.* Tasha couldn't deny Joe's swagger. He was definitely a fresh mu'fucka, and she felt like a fool for letting him slip through her fingers.

She shook thoughts of Joe from her brain and pulled out her cell phone to call Manolo. The phone rang several times before he answered.

"Hello?"

Tasha sighed. "Manolo, this is Tasha."

"What up? You and Amra cool?"

"Her moms is sick. She has cancer. And we don't have enough money to pay for her surgery. That's why I'm calling. Manolo, we need to borrow forty thousand dollars."

Manolo was silent for a minute.

"You know I wouldn't even be asking you this if I didn't really need it, and you know we're good for it." Tasha waited anxiously as Manolo contemplated the situation. *Say something*, she thought.

"Damn, forty gees is a lot of paper just to put up. I ain't even got it like that to even loan it to you, ma."

"That's all right, Manolo. You know I had to ask."

"I don't know if you gon' be down for this, but I know where you can get that cake."

"We'll do anything right about now. We just need to get the money to pay twenty-five percent of the bill. We'll worry about the rest later. If it can get us the money, we're with it."

"Let me take care of some of this business and find out a little bit more info for you. Make sure you and Amra come see me when y'all touch down in Flint."

"Thanks, Manolo. We'll be back tomorrow night."

Manolo could sense the relief in her voice. "No problem, baby. You know I got you."

Tasha hung up the phone, feeling like a huge burden had been lifted from her shoulders. She didn't know exactly what they had to do to get the money, but she knew they could get it done. Manolo hadn't led them astray yet, and she trusted him to put her up on a new hustle that would pay the type of money they were seeking.

Chapter Eleven

Tasha heard the doorbell ring, and Ms. Pat yelled up the stairs for her to come down. "Who the hell is here for me?" she asked herself as she descended the steps. She went to the door and saw Joe standing there waiting for her. He had on some Sean John jeans, a white T-shirt, all white Force One's, and a red fitted hat. Tasha smiled. "What are you doing here?" "I wanted to see you," he answered with a sexy grin.

Tasha folded her arms. "What about your girl?"

"I dropped her ass off. I told you, that's nothing. She was just something to do for the moment." Tasha frowned disapprovingly. "And what am I?" Joe neglected to answer the question. "You want to go for a ride?" Tasha looked down at the clothes she had on. She was wearing gray sweat pants and a pink Michigan State baby T-shirt. "Let me get dressed. You already saw me looking tore up earlier. I got to redeem myself."

"All right, I'll wait. Can I have a seat in the living room?"

"Sure. I'll be right back."

Tasha walked up the stairs and hurried into the room. She pulled out a mint green Christian Dior dress and applied her bronze makeup and fixed her hair. Excited to go out with Joe, she was dressed in under fifteen minutes. It had been a long time since they had spent time together. Just the simple fact that he had come over unannounced to see her made her think that he missed her.

By the time she re-entered the living room, Joe had already sweet-talked his way into Ms. Pat's good graces. Ms. Pat was smiling and laughing with Joe as if she had known him from the day he was born.

"I'm ready," Tasha stated as she walked into the room. The expression on Joe's face when he saw her confirmed what she already knew. She looked damn good. Tasha spun, to give him the full view.

"We all know you're gorgeous," Ms. Pat stated with a weak smile.

Tasha kissed Ms. Pat's cheek. "I won't be out too long."

"Don't worry about me. Spend some time with your friend." Ms. Pat then turned to Joe. "It was a pleasure meeting you, Joe. Make sure you come around again."

"I definitely will, Ms. Pat. Take care."

Tasha had to crack a smile as she followed Joe to his car. He had completely won Ms. Pat over. "Where are we going?" she asked.

Joe ignored her and turned up the volume to the music as they cruised down the block.

Tasha was quiet on the way there. She had a lot on her mind. She hadn't seen Joe in a long time and, for some reason, was nervous around him. She had changed a lot since they had last seen each other, and didn't know if he would like the new her.

They ended up at Sylvia's. Joe knew it was Tasha's favorite soul food spot, and one of the best in town.

As they sat over dinner, Tasha could feel Joe's eyes on her. "How you doing?" he asked her.

"I'm fine. Everything's good."

Joe didn't know exactly what was bothering her, but she wasn't acting the same. He reached across the table and grabbed her hands. "You cool? You need something?"

"No. All I need is you right now. It's good to see you. It seems like it's been forever." Tasha gave him a smile that melted his heart.

"So, when did you get back?"

"I just got here yesterday. Ms. Pat has cancer. We had to come and meet with some doctors."

Joe noticed the sadness in her tone as she spoke about Amra's mother. "I'm sorry to hear about that." He shook his head. "She seems like good people."

They finished their dinner in silence. Both of them seemed to just be satisfied with one another's company.

They were also unsure of how to approach one another. Joe admired the woman who sat in front of him, yet he couldn't figure her out. She seemed so confident, had the wit and sexiness of a mature woman despite her youthful age, but there was also sadness in her. He could tell she wanted to be with him, but for some reason, she was stopping herself from doing so.

When their dinner was complete, Joe said, "I want to take you somewhere." He drove her to an apartment building in Brooklyn, and they climbed up the fire escape, all the way to the top.

"What is this place?" Tasha asked, admiring the view of the city lights.

"I used to live in this building when I was little. I used to come up here and throw rocks at cars and shit," Joe said, reminiscing on his childhood years.

Tasha laughed softly. "Okay, bad ass."

Joe sat down on the edge of the rooftop and pulled Tasha close. "For real. I still come up here sometimes, you know, to clear my head when shit gets hectic."

Tasha leaned against him and relaxed for the first time in a long time. It felt good to lean against his strong body. It felt even better to be with a man she liked. Joe wasn't a job, he was just Joe. Naturally intrigued by his demeanor, she didn't have to pretend to be interested in him. There was something about him that made her heart flutter. She exhaled deeply and Joe held her tighter. "I missed you," Tasha admitted to him as she relaxed in his arms.

Joe didn't say anything. It felt good to have her in his arms. He'd thought about her a lot since she left, and he was glad she was safe and doing well.

Tasha tilted her head to look at him. She remembered she never could figure out what he was thinking. "Why do you do that? I can never figure you out. I never know how you are feeling."

Joe looked her directly in the eyes. "Words really don't mean shit, anyway. Me saying how I feel don't make it any more real than me showing you how I feel," he said in a low tone.

"That's just it. You don't show me either. I try to guess, but I don't know. I guess I just don't want to let myself feel something that's not really there. If I was sure that you felt the same way for me that I feel for you, I would have never gone to Flint."

"I know I'm not too good at this emotional stuff. I probably should've told you how I felt about you a long time ago, but this is all new to me. I've never had anybody give a damn about me. I've never loved anybody else but myself. Then you come along, and the feeling is so unfamiliar to me, I probably did handle you wrong. I'm not used to caring about another person. I never meant to confuse you, ma."

"You don't know how much shit I've gone through this past year. I'm not the same anymore," she whispered.

A tear escaped Tasha's eyes, and Joe trapped it with his thumb and brushed it away as he gripped her hair gently, bringing her face close to his. "Did somebody hurt you?" he asked, his voice becoming aggressive.

Tasha knew he would protect her if she needed him to. "No," she replied. "I don't want to talk about anything but us. I just want to be here right now with you."

He grabbed her face softly and kissed her gently on the lips, and Tasha kissed him back, firmly wanting to taste him. Her heart was beating fast. She'd already decided that if he tried to make love to her, she wasn't going to stop him.

Joe laid her on her back and started kissing her face, slowly working his way down her body. He unzipped the back of her dress and gently pulled it off of her perfect body. His kisses focused on her breasts, and she felt the tingles run up and down her spine as he gently sucked on her big brown nipples. He kissed her stomach, making his way to her thighs, lingering at her inner thigh.

Joe pulled off her black thong panties and simply kissed her clitoris as if he was kissing her mouth. He caressed her with his tongue, and she felt a sensation she had never experienced before. His hands felt good on her body, and his tongue felt even better inside of her.

Tasha arched her back and pulled him back up, wanting to see his face. She wanted him to tell her how he felt about her. She needed to hear three little words escape his mouth. She reached for his jeans and unbuttoned them. She felt his dick. It was hard, thick, and big, so she knew he would satisfy her completely. She crawled on top of him and worked her way down to his erect manhood, which was standing tall, and gently began to kiss it, starting at the tip and working her way down. Tasha had once said, "You will never catch a dick in my mouth!" but she loved Joe and just wanted to please him. She tried to take him into her mouth, but it was harder than she had expected.

Joe could tell she didn't know what she was doing, so he pulled her up and kissed her. He could tell that she was a virgin. It didn't bother him, though. He was actually happy about it. He took it slow, and gently put his manhood inside her.

Tasha flinched as he tried to penetrate her. It took a while because she was tight, and it hurt like hell as he tried to fit all of his ten inches into her virgin walls. When he finally did, she was wet as hell, and her pussy was tight, making the sex even better. He knew from the way it felt that she was indeed a virgin.

Tasha grimaced; it hurt badly with every stroke. She gripped his back tightly, and her nails dug into his back as he rocked gently in and out of her. The pain slowly transformed into pleasure as he thrust deeply inside of her. "I love you!" she whispered into his ear as he fucked her gently, making sure he wasn't hurting her.

Joe was well endowed, and the harder and deeper he explored, the better it felt.

Tasha climbed on top and straddled him, sitting on his dick, going all the way down until she was sure it had disappeared inside of her. She rode him slowly and loved being in control, especially when she saw the display of pure pleasure on his face.

Joe groaned. Tasha's pussy felt so good. He was fucking her raw, and felt like he was about to explode at any minute. She kissed him, and he smacked her ass as she rode him slowly. "Shit!" He grabbed her ass in a rough way.

Tasha could feel his dick starting to vibrate inside of her, and she rode the dick harder and faster. "Oh my . . . Joe . . ." She held on tight, and they both climaxed together.

She climbed off him, and he grabbed her and laid her on the hard cement floor of the rooftop. Tasha didn't care that they were on an abandoned building. The way Joe was treating her, she felt like she was in a five-star hotel.

Joe kissed her forehead. "I been wanting to show you that."

She laughed out loud and hit him playfully on the arm. "Joe, I do love you. I don't know why you never say it back, but that is the only reason why I left the first time. You wouldn't tell me what was up. I need you more than you know." She knew that Joe loved her. She just wanted to hear it. She put on her dress, and they fell asleep on the roof, holding each other tight.

Tasha's phone rang and woke her up. "Hello?" She tapped Joe to wake him up.

Amra said, "Tasha, where are you? Our plane leaves at four. I just wanted to make sure you remembered."

Tasha looked at the time on her phone. "It's only ten. I'll be there in a few. I want to make sure your moms is okay with us leaving before we go, anyway." She hung up.

Joe kissed her on the neck. She looked at him and said, "I have to go. I'm supposed to fly back to Flint today."

He looked at her and shook his head. "You don't have to go back there. Stay here. I'll take care of you. Anything you need, I got you."

"I want to. You don't know how bad I want to be with you."

"Then be with me. I got you. Just stay."

Tasha knew she couldn't stay in New York with Joe. She had to go back to Flint to make the money to pay for Ms. Pat's surgery. "I can't," she said in a whisper. "I have to take care of something in Flint. I don't want to, but I have to."

"Whatever it is, I'll take care of it."

Tasha shook her head. "You can't,"

Tasha knew that Joe didn't have $150,000 to just give away. He was balling, but not to the point where he could give her that much money.

When they got back to Ms. Pat's house, Tasha didn't want to get out of the car. Joe kissed her as if it was the last time he would see her. He pulled out a wad of money and handed it to her. "I love you too. Take care of yourself," he said to her as she got out of the car.

Tasha turned around and looked at Joe, and tears started to form in her eyes. "I will come back to you. That's my word." She kissed Joe again and walked into the house.

Joe had never told anybody that he loved them, but he knew that he loved her. It was something about Tasha. He always had known.

When Tasha got in the house, she rushed to the bathroom and collapsed against the door. Leaving Joe for a second time was hard. She knew what she had to do though, and the faster she went back to Flint to handle her business, the faster she could come back home and be with him.

Chapter Twelve

Detective Smith sat back in his chair, reviewing the criminal file laid out in front of him. He stared at the surveillance pictures that he and his partner had snapped the day before, and tried to think of a way he could take down various drug lords in the Flint area. Troy Smith didn't waste his time with the little guys either. No, he went after the big boys in the game. Over the last five years, he had put more major drug traffickers behind bars than any other narc or detective in FPD history. Born and raised in the 'hood, that gave him an advantage that the other cops hated him for. He didn't associate with other cops or detectives often, but he was well respected because of his accomplishments.

Smith took all of his investigations personally. His mother had been addicted to drugs and had eventually died from an overdose. There were many late nights that he saw his mother high, and heard her having sex with the dope man to pay him for his product. He still had childhood friends involved in the game, but he looked the other way because of loyalty. He couldn't arrest the same people that would have once taken a bullet for him, so he focused his attention on pushers that weren't from his old block. He had been a part of the game until he realized that he was on the wrong side of the law. Drugs were the very reason why his own mother wasn't alive, and when he was hustling, it bothered him that he might have been breaking up another family.

Smith worked as an undercover narcotics agent for many years, and was eventually promoted to detective after his success rate was recognized. His thuggish looks allowed him to infiltrate various drugs rings and eventually bring the operations down.

He had his eye on a couple of known dealers scattered throughout Flint's 'hoods. Of particular interest was one drug dealer named Keyshawn Keys, who for the last four years, reigned in the streets. Smith had been on his tail for years, but couldn't make anything stick. Keys had his shit wrapped tight and wasn't secretive about his profession either. He was cocky, but he was also smart. He had the streets on lock, and in the streets they called him "The New Teflon Don". No one would testify against him, and if someone actually cooperated with the authorities, they would mysteriously come up missing, quickly change their mind, or end up dead.

How can I take down this arrogant mu'fucka? Smith knew that there had to be a way to get Keys to slip up. He just hadn't found it yet.

Just as Smith began to put up the files he was viewing, his lieutenant, Jimmy Bonds, walked through the door. "What's up, Troy? How is the Keys investigation coming along? We need results. The captain is getting on my ass about this." Jimmy flopped down in Troy's desk chair.

"I can't even get an unpaid parking ticket on this cat. He doesn't slip up."

The lieutenant put both hands on Smith's desk. "I want you to set up surveillance on Key's house. I want his phones tapped, and a twenty-four-hour watch on his place. Let's keep this between us until you can get something concrete on him. He is flooding our streets with cocaine, and he is becoming untouchable."

"I'll get on it right away," Smith replied. The lieutenant exited the room, and Smith thought to himself, *The world would be a better place if we didn't have Keyshawn Keys running it.*

Troy Smith rode down North Saginaw Street and stopped on his old block to talk to some of his old friends that he had grown up with. He pulled up blasting Pac out of the subwoofers that sat in the back of his Chrysler 300. Smith hopped out of the car and immediately received love from his childhood friends who stood on the corner, trying to make their pay. He didn't agree with what they did, but they were trying to survive, and he understood that. He and his old friends had a mutual agreement. They let him know what was happening in the streets, and he let them know when they were getting hot and needed to lay low. He overlooked their wrongdoings to stay in tune with the streets. This helped Smith find out about incoming shipments and new faces on the scene that were making major moves.

"Yo', what up, kid?" one of the men on the corner yelled out as he and Smith showed each other love.

"What's good, Red?" Smith replied.

The man was smoking a blunt. He passed it to Smith, who took two long drags of the Mary Jane and gave it back. Smith looked at Red and whispered low, "Do we need to talk?"

Red looked around and nodded discreetly.

Smith jumped into his car and drove around the block, then parked on the curb.

A few minutes later, Red walked up and jumped in the car. "Aye, it's this new nigga in town. He is taking shit over. He makes Keys look like a nobody. I mean, he got some shit that's killing fiends. This nigga really got dope that's killing mu'fuckas. And them fiend-out mu'fuckas still want it. It's a demand on the street for what he got."

Smith rubbed his goatee. "Who is he? And where he be at?"

Red looked around nervously. Smith was his boy from back in the day, but he would never forget that he was also a cop. "I don't know too much about the nigga. Just that he goes by the name Jamaica, and is from New York. He doesn't even talk like he's from around here.

Um . . . oh yeah, he likes to go to the Coney Island spot on Corunna. You know, that place Atlas that be jumping after the club lets out."

Smith nodded and reached out his hand, and the guy slapped hands with Smith and jumped out of the car without saying another word.

Sounds like it's a new sheriff in town. Smith started his car and pulled off. He decided to roll by Atlas to see if he could get lucky and see this new cat they called Jamaica.

When he reached the restaurant, he parked his car and walked in. The place looked normal, people were talking, and nothing seemed out of the ordinary. He took a seat and ordered a slice of cheesecake and a coffee.

As he waited for the waiter to bring over his food, a group of men entered the diner. They were five deep, and all eyes glued to them as they entered. The group of men was obviously getting major dough. All of them were iced out with bling adorning their necks and wrists. Their pockets were fat, and they weren't trying to hide it. They took the booth right behind Smith and signaled for the waiter to come their way.

One guy stood out because of his expressionless face. He didn't smile, frown, or directly look at anyone. Obviously he was the head of the crew because he was the first to enter and the first to sit down.

The waiter brought Smith his cheesecake and coffee, and then moved over to the booth behind him and started to take orders. Smith could overhear the conversation, even though the men were almost whispering. Actually, he was eavesdropping.

"This ain't like back home. We got to stay low. I want to take over the South Side next."

Smith assumed he was the leader of the crew. When the waiter came to the table, the men stopped talking and got their drinks from him. Once he left, he began to speak again.

"Yeah, like I was saying, them niggas that's pushing coke that way got to make room. They got to get down or lay down."

One of the men added, "I know this chick that's fucking with one of them niggas. I think I might just be giving her a call tonight, Jamaica."

Smith almost choked on his cake when he heard him say "Jamaica". *Did he just say Jamaica?* Smith had heard all he needed to hear. He got up without finishing his cake and started to leave. He stared at the man they called Jamaica, and Jamaica stared right back at him. It seemed like it was in slow motion. The two men stared at each other like they had seen each other before. Once Smith passed him, he focused on the door as he exited the diner. *So that's Jamaica. That little nigga. He ain't no older than twenty-five. They are getting younger and younger. I know what he looks like now. He done fucked up.*

Chapter Thirteen

Tasha, Amra, Mimi, and Honey sat in front of Manolo as he admired their physical appearance. He had labeled his girls "The Manolo Mamis". There was no doubt in his mind that the women before him were the baddest bitches the game had ever seen, and he patted himself on the back for recruiting such a thorough group. Eventually, he would turn them out and pimp them full time, but for the time being, he was satisfied with the money they were making him just off the hustle.

Manolo took a liking to Tasha because her looks, street smarts, and natural intelligence put her far above the rest. Honey was coming in a close second, but she was conniving and manipulative. He knew that he couldn't trust her completely.

"Manolo, Amra and I are really in a bind. We need to come up in a major way. This is really life or death for us right now." Tasha thought of the burden of Ms. Pat's hospital bills.

"I think I got something for you, but the nigga is a murderer, and it's gon' be your ass if you fuck up."

Tasha looked around to see the reaction of her girls, but she didn't interrupt.

"His name is Keys, but it's gon' be a different type of hustle. You gon' just have to rob the nigga. He ain't caking it like these other dudes y'all been messing with. He ain't gon' be trying to spoil a bitch, nah mean? I know Keys. We came up together, and he got money sitting in a safe in his house."

Tasha didn't know if she would be able to rob somebody, especially not by herself. "Why can't I just get him to give me the money?" she asked.

"Keys ain't stupid. Nobody touches his money but him. The only way a bitch will ever get money out of Keys is if she's his wife, so you gon' have to do it my way. You gon' still get in good with him, like all the other times. Keys don't trust nobody, so you gon' have to get him to let you in his house. Once he trusts you enough to let you in, it's up to you to find out where the safe is at and get his combination. You gon' have to make this nigga love you. It can't be no funny shit. He can't see you or even hear about you fucking with another nigga, or he gon' drop you. He only fucks with real chicks. So, any dudes you keeping relations with gon' have to stop. Dead that shit now."

Tasha tried to absorb all the information that Manolo was telling her. The other girls were sitting there listening closely, knowing that at some point, they would have to help her.

"If he got his shit locked down like that, how do you know that I am going to even be able to get the combo to his safe? And even after all that, he ain't gon' never leave me at his crib alone, so when can I even get to the money?" Tasha wasn't afraid to hit a nigga, but she wasn't trying to get caught up in some hot shit either.

"You gon' have to keep your ears and eyes open. He handle a lot of business from home, so you gon' have to find a way. I didn't say that this was going to be easy. But Keys is the only nigga I know who got the kind of money you need. If you ain't with it—"

"I'm with it," she said. "How am I going to do this?" Tasha looked at Amra, who was praying that Tasha would do it.

Manolo left the room and came back with a picture of him and Keys. "This is him. Tomorrow night, you are going to go to the Fishbones in Detroit. He will be having dinner there with this woman named Eva. That's the woman that he's seeing now. I've been doing my homework, keeping tabs on the nigga. I've been watching him close. You will make eye contact there, make him interested in you. He has been fucking with Eva for about six months now, so you gon' have to knock her out the picture first. It's going to take him a minute to get back with you, if he even does. If he does, you see him as much as you can. Once you feel that you've gotten close enough to him, and once you've got the combination, get in contact with me, and I'll tell you what to do from there."

Amra stood up and said, "How long is this going to take, though? We need the money now."

"It's all on you. The quicker you get the combination, the faster you get paid."

"Who knows how long it's going to take him to trust her? We need the money now!" Amra yelled in distress.

Honey grabbed Amra's arm and hugged her. "Don't trip. Together, we all got enough money for the hospital to give your moms the surgery."

"Yeah, and when Tasha hits the safe, we'll just get it back then," Mimi added.

Manolo got up, signaling that the conversation was done. "Then it's settled. Tasha, you and Honey go to dinner tomorrow at the restaurant at seven o'clock."

The girls got up and left Manolo's house, unsure about how this would turn out.

"I don't know about this shit. I've heard of Keys before, and he ain't like none of these dudes out here. If he even thinks you trying to play him stupid, he is gonna fuck you up, Tasha," Mimi warned.

"I know, but he ain't gonna find out until it's too late."

Honey looked at Tasha with a worried expression. "Look, just be careful, okay?"

Each girl knew that this was the beginning of something serious. They had always used their looks and natural charms to get what they wanted; now they were getting straight grimy and taking what they needed.

I hope this doesn't blow up in my face. I hope everything goes okay. It has to go okay. I need to get this money for Ms. Pat. If I don't do this, then she is going to die. Tasha thought, anticipating the next day's events.

The next night, Tasha put on a short, gold Versace dress that fit her body tightly at the top and flowed loosely at the bottom. She applied a bronzer to her face, put mascara on her eyelashes, and lip-gloss on her lips. Amra was still asleep, so Tasha quietly crept out of the room and walked into Mimi's and Honey's room. Mimi was sitting on the bed, talking on her phone, and Honey was putting her makeup in her purse. "You ready?" Tasha asked.

Honey nodded her head, and they headed out of the door.

The girls took Tammy's car to Detroit. They both were silent on the way there, their nervous energy causing them to be at a loss for words.

After an hour-long drive, they pulled up to the restaurant. "You nervous?" Honey asked.

Tasha nodded and gave a weak smile. "Yeah, but it's time to put my game face on."

The girls got out of the car and walked into Fishbones as if they were big money like the other patrons in the five-star restaurant. They sat down at a candlelit table. The atmosphere was perfect for what they were trying to do.

Tasha looked around the restaurant, trying to find Keys, but he was nowhere to be found. The girls ordered their meals and impatiently ate their dinner.

Keys walked into the restaurant with a light-skinned woman.

"It shouldn't be that hard to snatch him from her," Honey commented.

Tasha looked at the tall high-yellow woman. She appeared to be around twenty-eight and wasn't all that special in Tasha's eyes. She wasn't ugly, but she wasn't a supermodel either. She looked like an average woman. "How am I supposed to make him notice me?" Tasha asked.

"Just wait," Honey replied. "You don't want to seem too eager. He needs to think you are meeting by chance."

Tasha nodded her head and finished eating her food. It was fun having dinner in an expensive restaurant with one of her best friends.

Honey looked up from her plate and noticed that Keys was staring over at them. "Don't look now, but I think you grabbed your boy's attention," she stated.

Tasha smiled, making sure that it was one of the best smiles she ever displayed.

Honey laughed quietly. "Got him! Girl, his eyes are glued over here."

Tasha looked up too, and Keys subtly winked his eye at her. She didn't expect for him to be so debonair. His style was intriguing in itself, and on top of his looks, he was a perfect ten.

"Damn!" Honey said, referring to Keys' looks. He was dark-skinned, with a body to die for. He had a dimple in his left cheek, and the demeanor of a thug. He was sexy in every sense of the word.

Tasha watched as Keys' date got up and went to the bathroom.

"Excuse me, waiter," Honey said, signaling the waiter to come over to their table. When the waiter came over, Honey asked, "Can you deliver a note over to that man's table right there?"

The waiter responded, "Certainly."

Tasha used her napkin and wrote, *I don't usually do this. 810-785-0810. Tasha*

Tasha slipped the waiter a twenty-dollar tip and watched as he delivered the note to Keys' table. When he got it, he read it and looked at Tasha, who raised her wineglass to him, and he raised his back.

Tasha took a sip of her wine, and then paid the bill as Keys' date came back to the table. Tasha and Honey walked past the couple and out the door. Tasha knew that Keys was watching her, so she turned around and gave him a gorgeous smile before she left.

Three days days passed before Tasha received a phone call from Keys. "Yo', this Keys. I sort of met you the other night at Fishbones."

Tasha smiled to herself, relieved he had finally called her. "Oh, I remember. I didn't think you would call."

Keys laughed softly. "Nah, you were intriguing. I had to call you. I'm trying to see what you're about."

Tasha had to admit to herself that he was charming.

"I want to see you," he said.

She was shocked that he wanted to meet face to face. The way that Manolo had described him, Keys seemed like he was hard to get close to.

"Okay, you tell me when and where."

"Next Monday. I want to take you out for the day."

Tasha agreed and hung up the call.

Monday came, and Keys picked Tasha up. She walked out of the house looking radiant. She had on a black Dolce & Gabbana pants suit, and the jacket opened just below her breasts, exposing her flat stomach and wide hips. She had on silver Manolo Blahnik shoes and jewelry from Tiffany's. She knew that she would have Keys open on just her appearance alone.

When Keys saw her, he was positive that she was the most beautiful woman he had ever seen. He couldn't take his eyes off of her.

Tasha walked over to his black Mercedes Benz and got in. She knew he was getting money, because not many people in Flint whipped a Benz. "Hi," she said sweetly when she sat down in the passenger seat.

Keys nodded his head and drove off.

That first day, he took her everywhere. They spent the day together, talking and laughing about everything. He was softer than she expected, and was glad that Manolo was wrong. They saw each other every day after that, and she enjoyed spending time with him.

Only a couple of weeks had passed, but she and Keys were cool. They had fun together, and Tasha made him forget about the things that were bothering him.

"I need a favor," he said to her as he watched her eat the salad she'd ordered.

She looked up and said, "What's that?"

Keys pulled out two tickets to Chicago. "Come away with me for a while."

Tasha looked at the tickets, and then confusion spread across her face. "What's 'a while', Keys? How long?"

"A month."

Tasha laughed. "I can't go away with you for a month, Keys. I have a salon to run. And my friends, I don't . . . I don't know. I just can't. I barely know you."

Keys reached across the table and grabbed Tasha's hands. "Tasha, I'm leaving town for a little while. I want you to come with me. I'll give you whatever you want. I know we just met, but I don't want to leave you behind. I want you to come with me so that I can get to know you better."

Tasha knew that if she didn't go to Chicago with Keys that he would forget about her, and she would be replaced just as easily as she had replaced the woman before her. She needed to prove to him that she was loyal. If he trusted her to go out of town with him, then when they got back, he would trust her in his home.

"Okay, I'll go. When do we leave?"

Keys smiled and sat back in his chair. "Tomorrow."

"Tomorrow!" Amra exclaimed out loud when Tasha delivered the news to her friends.

"Damn! Why he got to go to Chicago, anyway?" Mimi asked.

Tasha shrugged her shoulders. "I don't know, but I'm going. If I don't, then there is no way I'm gonna be able to get the money from him."

Honey stood with her hands on her hips. "Well, let's get you packed."

"I don't have to pack. He's going to buy me clothes when we get there." Tasha smiled.

"Damn! You got it like that?" Mimi exclaimed.

"The nigga's nose is wide the fuck open." Tasha walked out of the room. She remembered the reason why she was doing all this. She pulled out her cell and called Ms. Pat.

"Hello?" Ms. Pat answered weakly.

"Hi, it's me. I was just wondering how you were feeling."

"Oh, I'm doing fine."

Tasha could hear from the tone of her voice that she wasn't doing fine. "I'm gonna get the money for your surgery," Tasha said, trying to reassure Ms. Pat that she was going to be all right.

"Don't worry about me, sweetheart. I am going to be just fine. I have two girls that I love, and even though I didn't give birth to you, I still love you like you are my own."

Tasha felt the tears build in her eyes. "I love you too, Ms. Pat," she replied before hanging up the phone.

The next day, Keys was at her house early to pick her up. "You ready?" he asked as he opened the car door for her.

Tasha nodded her head yes, and waved to her friends, who were watching in the doorway.

The flight to Chicago wasn't long, but Tasha slept the entire way there. When they finally arrived, Keys checked them into a five-star hotel near downtown.

"You need anything?"

Tasha shook her head no.

Keys pulled off his shirt and walked over to the bed and lay down on his back.

Tasha stood near the door, feeling a bit awkward about being alone with him for so long. "So, what are we doing tonight?" she asked sweetly as she walked over and sat down next to him.

"Whatever you want to do."

"I really just want to relax."

Keys wanted to cater to her every need, so that night, he arranged for them to receive a spa treatment from the hotel facilities. He paid for her to have a massage, a mud bath, a facial, and a manicure. Tasha basically got a full makeover, and she loved every minute of it. *I could get used to this shit,* she thought to herself.

The days seemed to fly by as Keys courted her around the city of Chicago. He took her shopping, they ate out at five-star restaurants every night, and he treated her like his queen. Tasha enjoyed the treatment, but she was worried about Ms. Pat and couldn't wait to get the money for her surgery. She didn't want to steal from Keys, especially since he was treating her so well, but Ms. Pat was hanging on by a thread.

Some nights, Keys had business to tend to, so Tasha was left alone in the hotel. These nights were good nights, because she got time to call her friends and check on them. For some reason, spending time with Keys made her think of Joe. She loved Joe, but she didn't know how long he would wait for her. Tasha couldn't wait to get back to Flint. *The quicker I finish this, the quicker I can get to Joe.*

On their last night in Chicago, Keys sat Tasha down and said, "I'm glad you came here with me."

"Me too. " Tasha smiled. "I had fun with you."

Keys grabbed Tasha's face and kissed her softly on the lips.

She had him right where she needed him to be. *When we get back to Flint, I'm gonna get this money. I hope it won't be too hard to find out the combo to his safe.*

The night they flew back into Flint, Keys immediately took her to his lavish house in the suburbs. It was big as hell, and it definitely flaunted the amount of money he had. The house had seven bedrooms and was laced on the inside and out. *This nigga definitely got deep pockets.* Tasha observed all the high-priced shit that filled the living room.

Keys led her to his bedroom, and as soon as she stepped in, he pinned her against the wall and started kissing her on the neck. He was all over her as if he hadn't had a shot of pussy in years. Tasha hadn't fucked Keys while they were in Chicago, and he never pressured her. Keys wanted her to be comfortable with him first. Tasha was definitely not comfortable though. She didn't want to have sex with him, but she knew that if she refused him, he would not fuck with her.

Keys ripped off her shirt and began to suck on her nipples. Tasha frowned because he was sucking so hard. He was rough with her and she didn't like it, but she didn't let him know that.

"Yeah, girl, I'm 'bout to tear this shit up!" he whispered in a low, raspy tone as he followed her to the bed.

Tasha lay down on the bed and reluctantly spread her legs. Tears formed in her eyes, and she quickly wiped them away. Joe had been the only man that she had given herself to, and she didn't want to add Keys to the list. *Just get through this. Think about something else,* she told herself.

"I'm about to tear that shit up!" Keys screamed. He was like a pit bull. He kicked off his jeans and pulled off his boxers.

Tasha lifted her head and looked at his muscular body. He definitely had a good physique. His body was easy on the eyes. Her eyes started at his chest, and then made their way down to his washboard abs and perfectly chiseled arms. Her eyes slowly drifted down and—*that's it?* Tasha couldn't believe his dick was so little. His balls didn't even hang; they were like two little bloated raisins. *Little, short, fat, breakfast-sausage-dick-having* . . . she had to stop herself from laughing.

Keys climbed on top of her and humped away. Tasha was practically still a virgin, and she still didn't feel a thing. Keys was enjoying himself though, and that's all that mattered.

"Yeah, girl, you like that?"

Tasha gave a fake performance, trying to make Keys think he was the best she'd ever had. She moaned like a porn star, hoping it would help him finish faster.

Keys finally climaxed, and Tasha turned around and pretended to go to sleep. *Please don't say anything to me,* she thought to herself, not wanting to talk to him. He kissed her on her cheek, and she cringed when his lips touched her skin.

The phone rang abruptly, and Keys reached over to the nightstand to answer it. "Yo'."

Tasha opened her eyes and listened attentively.

"Yeah, I got it. When you need it?" Keys listened. "I'll get that for you tomorrow. Make sure you have my money, nigga," he stated harshly, before hanging up the phone.

She felt Keys get out of the bed, and heard him walk over to the wall. She turned around and saw him take a picture off the wall, revealing the safe behind it. Tasha strained her eyes to see the numbers Keys was opening his safe with—*thirty-four . . . seventeen . . . twenty.* He turned around, and Tasha quickly closed her eyes. She made a mental note of the numbers, and turned around and went to sleep with a huge smile on her face. *It's game time, baby!*

Chapter Fourteen

"Don't use yo' teeth, ma," Keys said, frustrated, as Tasha kneeled in front of him. "Just go slow. You act like you never sucked dick before."

Tasha thought to herself, *That's because I haven't.* She began blowing Keys as he held the back of her head and guided her every movement. She tried to stop herself from gagging, but she couldn't help it. She didn't want this nigga's dick in her mouth, and the disgust showed in her performance.

Keys threw his head back and looked down, watching his dick appear and then disappear over and over.

Tasha had never given anyone a blowjob before, and she really wasn't feeling it either. She thought to herself, *I have to get this money, and I will do whatever I got to do to get it. This will be over soon.*

Just as Tasha completed her thought, Keys climaxed on her chest, and lay back on the sofa.

Disgusted with herself, Tasha got off her knees and walked into the bathroom. She ran hot water and practically scalded her mouth, trying to get the taste of him out of it. She wiped her face and looked in the mirror, contemplating. She was nervous as hell, and her hands wouldn't stop shaking. *Should I do this? I don't know if I can do this.*

She had come too far to turn back now. She reached into her bra and pulled out the two pills Manolo had given her to put in Keys' drink. She looked at the pills and said in a low voice, "I hope this shit keeps you knocked out long enough."

"You all right in there!" Keyes yelled loudly.

The sound of his voice startled her, causing her to drop the pills. *Oh shit!* She watched as one of the pills fell into the sink and went down the drain in slow motion. She reached down to try to grab it, but it was too late. "Fuck!" She tried to stick her finger down the small dark hole. *What the fuck am I supposed to do now? I only have one pill left.* Tasha placed the remaining pill back in her bra. She hoped it would be enough to get the job done.

Tasha walked out and saw Keys sitting on the sofa, zipping up his jeans. He looked at her. "I knew I felt something between me and you. The first time I saw you I was feeling you, Tasha."

Tasha smiled and walked into his kitchen. "I hope you ain't done yet. I want to feel you inside of me." Tasha needed him to want her. The more distracted he was, the better chance she had of slipping him a mickey.

Keys stood up and walked over to Tasha. He began to kiss her neck.

Tasha leaned back. "Slow down. Let's have a couple of drinks first. It'll loosen me up and get me in the mood."

"Cool. I got some Henny in the cabinet and some champagne in the cellar."

Tasha placed her finger on his lips and kissed him softly. "Let me take care of that. You just go and get ready," she whispered seductively.

Keys started to walk backward out of the kitchen, keeping eye contact with Tasha, and licking his lips. She could see his dick getting hard again as he thought about her, and it almost made her throw up.

As soon as he exited the kitchen, Tasha took a deep breath, trying to calm herself. Her stomach was in knots. She knew Keys would kill her if he thought she was trying to do something grimy.

She turned toward the cabinet, pulled out two wineglasses, and walked toward the refrigerator. She poured two glasses of champagne and dropped the "roofie" into one of the glasses. She stuck her finger in the glass and stirred it up, and the pill quickly dissolved.

Tasha picked up the spiked glass with her right hand, so she wouldn't mix them up, and walked into Keys' bedroom, where he was stripped down to his boxers. When she walked in, he motioned for her to come over to the bed. She handed Keys the drink, and he quickly placed it on the night-stand.

"Come on, ma. Come get me right again."

Tasha smiled and grabbed his drink and hand-ed it to him. "Let's have a drink first. I need to get more relaxed."

Keys sighed in frustration and picked up his glass.

Tasha unbuttoned her shirt and raised her wineglass. "To us!" she said. Keys touched glass-es with her, and they both began to drink.

Tasha only took a sip of her champagne, want-ing to have a clear head for what she was about to do. She eyed Keys as she impatiently waited for the drug to take its affect. *He doesn't even seem affected. It should have knocked his ass out by now.*

She put down her drink as Keys finished his, stood up, and started to undress herself, waiting for the drug to take its course. *Come on, pass the fuck out!* Tasha thought as she danced for him, giving him a striptease.

Keys put his hands on her hips as she rolled her body in a teasing way. He attempted to stand up and instantly became woozy. "Damn, ma, I don't feel too—" He was out before he could finish the sentence.

"It's about damn time!" she said.

The drug had taken longer to start working than Tasha expected. Her heart felt as if it would beat out of her chest. She quickly put her clothes back on and ran to the front window to signal the girls. She opened and closed the blinds repeatedly to alert them. A couple minutes later, her friends were at the door.

Honey was the last to walk in. "Tasha, is he out?"

Tasha nodded. "We have to hurry up for real! I only gave him one of the pills. I dropped the other one down the sink."

Honey stayed in the front room, while Amra and Tasha headed toward the safe in the bedroom. Tasha hurried over to the safe, and Amra stood by the door, keeping her eyes on Keys. "Tasha, hurry up!" Amra said.

"I know. I'm trying." Tasha took the painting off the wall and began to think. *Thirty-four, seventeen, twenty . . . I think.* She began to try to open the safe.

Keys started to move.

Tasha looked back at him. *The pill is wearing off!* She began to shake nervously, messing up her concentration. She had to start over and put the combination in again. "Fuck!" Tasha shouted to herself.

"Hurry up, Tasha!" Amra whispered nervously. "He's waking up!"

Tasha's hands were sweaty, and she couldn't get the combination to save her life. "Come on!" she yelled to herself.

At that moment, Keys sat up, trying to focus his blurred vision on Tasha. "What the fuck is going on, bitch?" He yelled out loud. His body felt heavy as he tried to gather himself.

Tasha quickly turned around and was speechless.

"You trying to rob me, bitch!" He tried to stand up, but he could barely keep his eyes open, and his legs were weak. He could not keep himself up. He sloppily reached under his bed and pulled a gun.

Tasha was frozen in fear, and Amra did not move, realizing that Keys didn't know she was in the doorway.

Keys pointed the gun at Tasha and fired a shot. Tasha screamed in fear as the bullet flew by her shoulder blade. She grabbed her shoulder and realized she wasn't hit.

Keys, barely able to aim his gun, fired a second shot and missed Tasha by an inch. He aimlessly pointed the gun again, but before he could pull the trigger, Amra grabbed the brass lamp that sat on the dresser and hit him in the head from behind.

He immediately dropped the gun, and grabbed the back of his head and yelled out in pain, "Fuck!"

Amra hit him repeatedly, bringing the lamp up above her head and smashing it down forcefully over Keys' head. She dropped the lamp when she saw the blood begin to seep from the back of his head. "Hurry up! Hurry!" she said over and over again as Keys started to regain his composure as each second passed by.

Tasha was shaking. The more she tried, the harder it was for her to steady her hand enough for her to open the safe. "I can't!" Tasha screamed.

Keys got up from the floor. "You dirty-ass bitch!" He turned around and slapped Amra hard across the face, causing her to fall to the floor.

Tasha was frozen in place as Keys put his hands around Amra's neck. Tasha didn't know what to do, everything was happening so fast. Her first reaction was to pick up his gun from the floor, but instead, she went for the brass lamp.

"Get the fuck off of her!" Tasha brought the lamp above her head and brought it crashing down on Keys. She felt the impact of the hit; she heard something crack beneath his skull. She raised the lamp again and hit him a second time to make sure he wouldn't get up anytime soon. Keys' body collapsed on top of Amra, and large amounts of blood began to flow onto her.

"Amra, let's go! We have to get out of here!" Tasha helped her friend up. She looked down at Keys' body, and the sight of what she had done made her sick to her stomach. *I killed him!* Her stomach started to feel like jello, and her feet felt like they weighed a ton. She just stood there shaking and terrified, her mouth fixed wide open in a state of shock. So many different things raced through her head, and she didn't know what to do next. "Is he dead?" She looked at Amra, now still from disbelief.

Amra nodded her head up and down. "I don't know. I don't know. It all happened so fast."

Tasha paced the room and yelled, "No, no, no! This shit was not supposed to happen." She knelt against the wall and put her face into her head.

Honey ran into the room. She wanted to see what was taking so long. "What happened?" She saw the blood oozing from the back of Keys' head. "Oh God!" she yelled. "Get the money so we can get the fuck out of here!"

Tasha opened the safe, and it was full of cash. Actually, it was more than she thought. He had stashed all hundreds in the safe. She wasn't sure how much it was, but it had to be at least a hundred thousand dollars. Honey threw her a pillowcase, and she quickly started to fill it up.

Honey took a look at Keys and asked Tasha, "Is he dead?"

"I think so, but I didn't mean to kill him."

Amra sat in the corner of the room, her knees tucked to her chest, staring at Keys' body. She had a blank expression on her face as she rocked back and forth.

Honey told Tasha, "Check to see if he's breathing."

"Bitch, you check him."

"Fuck it! Let's just go."

Tasha could feel herself getting ready to panic.

"Okay, okay, um . . . wipe off everything you touched, and let's get the fuck out of here."

Tasha got up and reached for the wineglass that she had earlier and quickly began to wipe it clean with one of Keys' T-shirts. She then hurried over to the safe and wiped the handle and combination knob down. Once she was finished, she helped Amra up off the floor, and they all headed for the door.

Mimi was in the car waiting for them, the car running and the lights shut off. The girls jumped in the car, and Honey yelled, "Go!"

Tasha pulled out her cell phone and tried to call Manolo. Her hands were shaking so badly that she couldn't even dial the number straight.

Amra screamed from the back seat, "What the fuck just happened? This is not what we planned. That wasn't supposed to go down like that." She began to cry.

Honey turned around and looked at her. "Yo', Amra, we're going to be okay. Just relax. I'm going to call Manolo. He'll know what to do."

Tasha reached her hand out and grabbed Amra's face. "Everything is going to be okay. Just calm down, okay?" She wanted to believe what she had just told Amra, but she knew they had just gotten themselves into some shit.

Amra nodded her head up and down.

When the girls made it back to the house, Tammy was just leaving. "Hey, girls. I might not be home tonight," she said as she exited the house with a male friend.

Honey and Tasha said, "Okay," in unison, and they hurried into the house, pulling Amra along. The girls went into the living room and sat down.

"What next?" Amra looked at Tasha.

"We fucked up," Tasha admitted.

Honey looked at each one of her friends. "If you didn't kill him, he would have killed Amra. You did what you had to do, plain and simple. Keys had too many enemies for this shit to fall back on us. Nobody saw us go in, and nobody saw us come out. We're straight." Honey grabbed the sack of money and dumped the pillowcase out onto the center table. The room was quiet as they all looked at the money on the table.

Honey suddenly yelled, "*Wooohooo!*" and grabbed a fistful of money and began to count it.

It seemed as if everyone's mood changed when they saw the money. Mimi stood up, and a huge smile crossed her face. All the girls joined in and grabbed handfuls of money and threw them into the air, making money fall from the ceiling like confetti.

Tasha looked over at Amra, and noticed that she had the same look on her face that she had at Keys' house. Tasha grabbed some cash and waved it in her face. "Amra, it's all over now. We paid. We can take care of your mom's bills."

Amra looked into Tasha's eyes, then looked at the money, and slowly cracked a smile as she grabbed some of it and slowly began to swim her fingers through it.

Tasha yelled, "Hold on, everybody. Let's call Manolo, and then count this shit up."

Honey was in a zone. It was like she didn't even hear Tasha. She was too busy counting the money and softly singing a Biggie song. She was already planning what she would do with the cash.

Tasha finally got her attention and said, "Let's count this shit up and take out the money for Ms. Pat first. Then we will split the rest."

Honey looked up and replied, "Cool."

They began to count the money.

Tasha called Manolo, but didn't tell him about what happened at Key's house.

"So, y'all got the money?" he asked her.

"Yeah, we got it."

After Tasha hung up the phone, she helped Honey count out the money, while Mimi and Amra just sat and watched.

"Let's count it again."

"Tasha, we just counted this shit five times already. It's only one hundred and sixty grand here." Honey leaned back in her chair and looked at the twenty different stacks of hundred-dollar bills sitting on the table in front of her.

Tasha said, "Ms. Pat can get her surgery." She looked over at Amra and Mimi, who had both fallen asleep on the couch. "We did it, Honey. I was worried about how I was gon' get this money for Ms. Pat, but I got it."

Honey responded with less enthusiasm. "Yeah, we did it, but was it worth the price? A man is dead because of us."

Tasha's enthusiasm went from high to low instantly. It was almost as if she had forgotten what had just taken place a couple of hours earlier. "We need to go see Manolo in the morning. I didn't tell him about Keys."

Honey shook her head. "Good. He doesn't need to know that we fucked up."

"I'm done with this shit. We just killed a man, Honey. After we talk to Manolo, I'm out. I'm going back home. Besides, Joe is there, and I want to be there with him. We ain't nothing but gold diggers, and that shit has gotten old real quick. Eventually, all this grimy shit we doing is going to catch up with us." Tasha paused for a minute, thinking about all the shit she'd done since coming to Flint.

Honey knew exactly how her friend felt, but instead of agreeing she said, "Help me put the money away. I'm tired." Honey began to put the money in the pillowcase with Tasha's help.

As Tasha lay in bed, she couldn't get the image of Keys' body sprawled on the bed out of her mind. She tossed and turned, trying to focus on something else—anything that would take her mind to a peaceful place. She had never seen a dead body before. *I helped kill someone,* she thought to herself as tears ran down her cheeks.

Eventually she fell asleep, Keys' death haunting her conscience.

Chapter Fifteen

Early the next day, the girls grabbed the money they'd stolen from Keys and headed to Manolo's house. The events of the night before had their minds racing.

I can't believe that he's dead. I helped kill Keys. Eventually, somebody is going to find his body. I know I didn't wipe all my fingerprints from out of his house. I was all over the place. I couldn't have gotten every one of them. How did I get myself into this? Tasha was overwhelmed with fear, anxiety, and pain.

Amra was shaken. If they got caught, she and Tasha would be the ones to get the worst punishment. *I didn't try to kill him. I have to get out of Flint before they find Keys' body. I can't go to jail. They all acting like everything's normal. Keys was a boss. If the police don't get us, somebody will.*

Mimi looked at Amra and could see she was deep in thought. She knew she couldn't be tied into what had happened inside Keys' house, so she wasn't tripping. *Shit, I wasn't in the house when they killed Keys, so I don't really give a fuck. My prints ain't there or nothing, so I'm straight. Fuck what they talking about!*

Honey's mind had been blank ever since they'd left Keys' house. *We messed up. It should never have gotten to that level. Tasha should have given him both pills. We did all this, and we still don't get to keep no money. Ain't that a bitch?*

When the girls arrived at Manolo's house, they were all solemn and confused.

Manolo picked up on their vibe as soon as they entered his house. "What's wrong? Y'all got the money, right?"

Tasha spoke up first. "We cool. The money's right here." She placed the duffel bag full of money on the table.

Manolo began to count it. It took him a minute. As soon as he was done, he announced, "One hundred and fifty thousand."

Tasha frowned her face in confusion and turned to look at Honey. Honey winked her eye, and Tasha knew her girl had pocketed the extra ten gees.

"So, how much does your moms surgery cost?" Manolo asked, looking at Amra.

She doesn't look too good, Tasha thought to herself, assuming Amra was still sick about the night before.

Amra sat down next to Manolo and said, "Her surgery is a hundred and fifty thousand."

Manolo shook his head and started putting the money back in the bag. "Here. Take it and take care of her."

Amra looked up at Tasha, and then back at Manolo. "You're not going to take a cut?"

Manolo shook his head. "You won't have enough to handle your business if I take my cut."

Amra hugged Manolo tightly. "Thank you so much, Manolo. You don't know how much you are doing."

"Oh, I ain't doing this out of the kindness of my heart," he quickly replied. "I got another job for y'all."

Tasha cut in. "I can't do that shit no more, Manolo. I'm sick of this hustle. It's getting old."

Honey added, "Yeah, we done with that."

Manolo shook his head. "Fuck that! I need y'all to do this job for me. Y'all owe me, as much shit as I've done for you. Or y'all can give me my cut from the Keys job, and we'll call it even." Manolo was calm. He didn't get loud or anything, but he made it clear that they were going to do this for him. He knew they couldn't afford to give him a cut of the money because of Ms. Pat's surgery, so he had them right where he wanted them. Their silence was his cue to continue.

"It's not the type of job that you're used to, though. This is a one-time thing. And it's going down the day after tomorrow."

Tasha didn't care what type of job it was. Whatever it was, she wasn't down with it. "I'm not doing it. I told you, I can't fuck with that shit anymore," she said in a shaky voice, remembering how she felt when she saw Keys fall onto his floor, his head bleeding.

Manolo sat back on the couch and stared Tasha in the eye. "I need all four of y'all for this. I looked out for you when I didn't take my cut out of the hundred and fifty gees. Now you need to look out for me with this."

Tasha rolled her eyes at Manolo and sat down in the chair farthest from him. "Fine, but after this, don't ask me to do nothing else, because I'm done. This is the last time."

Manolo nodded his head. "I need y'all to deliver a package for me. I need y'all to deliver some dope to my cousin down in Florida. I can't get it through the airport, but y'all can."

"Hell nah!" Mimi stated, shaking her head. "If we get caught with dope in the airport, that's a fucking felony."

Manolo quickly replied, "You won't get caught."

"Well, why can't you do it yourself, if it's no chance of getting caught?" Honey asked.

Manolo had been expecting them to ask him questions. He knew they weren't dumb, and he would have to talk them into doing it. "I'm a black man. I'm guaranteed to get searched. They won't search y'all."

Amra stood up and walked toward the door. "I'm not doing that shit."

Tasha dropped her head, knowing they didn't have a choice. "We have to," she said quietly. She turned her attention toward Manolo. "What do we do?"

Manolo smiled mischievously and rubbed his hands together. "Just deliver the package and pick up the money and bring it back. Your flight leaves out of Bishop Airport the day after tomorrow at ten in the morning. Come to my house that morning at six o'clock."

Honey asked, "How are we supposed to get drugs through a damn airport?"

"You'll see when you come over that morning."

The girls, pissed off that Manolo had pulled them into something so hot, got up and left the house. When they finally arrived home, they passed out in their beds. They were tired, and upset.

Tasha went to sleep. Her dreams seemed like the only place she could get away. Since the day she had arrived in Flint, she had been doing things she wouldn't normally do. She was exhausted from partying every night, paranoid from the thought of being caught by the police for Keys' murder, and homesick from being away from Joe.

The next morning, Tasha woke up and walked downstairs, where Tammy was making breakfast. She took a seat at the table.

"Hey, Tasha," Tammy said. "Are you hungry?"

"Yeah. Thanks, Tammy."

Tammy placed a plate in front of Tasha, and she sat and ate breakfast with Honey, Mimi, and Tammy. Amra was still asleep.

"Is Amra doing all right? She hasn't been looking too good lately," Tammy commented.

"Yeah, she'll be okay." Tasha got up from the table and fixed Amra a plate of food. She walked up to the room that she shared with Amra, who was tucked underneath her covers.

Tasha pulled back the covers and noticed that Amra's skin was blotchy and her eyes were dark around the lids. "Amra, wake up. You need to eat something. You haven't eaten much lately."

Amra groggily sat up in her bed. "I'm not hungry."

"What's wrong with you?"

Amra shook her head and started to cry. "I can't do this shit no more, Tasha. I'm ready to just go home. We need to hurry and go back home, so my momma can have her surgery. I'm not trying to do no more grimy shit. I just want to go be with her."

"We're going back to home as soon as we do this last job for Manolo. We'll be back home by next week." Tasha hugged Amra and left the food on the stand by the bed. "Eat something, okay?"

Amra nodded her head and wiped her eyes, and then Tasha walked out the door.

The day crept by slowly, giving the girls too much time to think. Tasha couldn't wait until she was back in New York. *I just want to be with Joe,* she thought to herself as she remembered the night she'd spent with him. It had been months, and she just wanted to hurry up and get back to him.

She made her way to Honey's room and sat on the bed across from her.

"Close the door," Honey told her.

Tasha got up and closed the bedroom door, and then asked, "What's up?"

Honey pulled out the ten thousand dollars she had taken from the money that was in Keys' safe. She counted out five thousand dollars and handed it to Tasha.

"I don't want to do this thing with Manolo."

Honey nodded her head. "I know, but what else is there to do?"

Tasha didn't answer. She just walked out of the room and walked into her own, and then went to sleep.

The next morning, all of the girls headed to Manolo's place. The ride was quiet, and the anticipation of what they were about to do grew more and more during the ride. The girls arrived at Manolo's house, and he greeted them at the door. He felt the animosity from them, but it didn't bother him. *They owe me. I don't give a fuck if they want to do it or not.*

Once all of the girls were in and seated, Manolo pulled out a duffel bag from behind the couch. He opened the bag and pulled out duct tape and eight white packages. He then walked into the back room and returned with an arm full of clothes. "All right, this is how it's going down. I'm going to strap y'all with the dope, and my cousin will meet y'all at the airport in Florida. He's going to give you two briefcases full of money and plane tickets to a flight that comes back the next day." Manolo started searching through his pile of clothes. "Who's first?"

Mimi stood up, and he gave her a corny outfit. "I ain't wearing this ugly shit!" she said.

"Mimi, be smart. This is not a fashion show. We trying to move weight."

Mimi quickly changed her attitude.

"Take off your shirt."

Mimi looked at Manolo like he was crazy. "What?"

"Take off your shirt. I've seen titties before."

After Mimi reluctantly took off her shirt, Manolo began to strap the dope to her chest, wrapping it firmly.

Thirty minutes later, Manolo had taped all of the girls. As he escorted them to the airport, he briefly went over the small details of the task. "Be calm. It's going to be easy. Just don't seem nervous."

It seemed like the girls became more nervous when he said that.

"My cousin is going to take y'all to a hotel. Just give him the drugs, and he'll give you the money. He's family, so don't worry about anything."

They finally reached the airport. Just before they exited the car, Manolo grabbed Honey's arm just as she was getting out, and whispered, "Don't fuck with me!"

Honey smiled at Manolo. "You know we don't even get down like that. We would never try to get over on you."

Tasha, Honey, Amra, and Mimi entered the airport, walking side by side. All of them could sense the other's nervousness, but no one said a word. They each had a pit in their stomach, and they were growing uneasy as the minutes passed by. Without looking at each other, they separated, each going a different way, as if they didn't even know each other.

Tasha's appearance was far from her usual attire. She wore a yellow sundress with yellow flip-flops, and the dope that was taped in place around her stomach made it look like she was at least five months pregnant. She had on a pair of sunglasses that covered most of her upper face. She was glad that something covered her eyes, because she knew that if someone were to look into them, they would see how nervous she was. She was breathing hard, and the palms of her hands were sweating profusely. She kept looking around. It felt like everybody in the airport was looking her way.

The lady that sat next to her looked at her with concern. "Miss, are you okay? Do you need some water?"

Tasha shook her head no, and put her hands on her stomach, patting her "baby". "No, thank you. I just get short-winded sometimes." She got up and hurried to the bathroom. She felt

the plastic dope package stick against her skin.
*I can't do this. I'm never gonna make it on that
plane with this stuff.*

Tasha stood in the mirror and set her luggage
down. She grabbed a paper towel, wet it, and
then patted it against her face, trying to gather
herself. She was shaking from paranoia. She had
to control herself, or she was going to be a dead
giveaway. Sweat started to form on her skin from
the plastic bags taped around her. It was uncomfortable, and she was trying her best to appear
to be a pregnant woman. She turned to the side
and studied her stomach to make sure that she
didn't look too bulky. She took a deep breath in
the mirror, and picked up her luggage. She exited the restroom and went back to her terminal,
where she waited to board her flight.

Mimi, in a long jean skirt and a W.W.J.D.
T-shirt, sat with a Bible in her left hand and
her suitcase in the other. Every time she saw a
security guard, she thought they were coming
for her. *Calm down. You can do this,* she told
herself as she sat there clenching the Bible. She
felt the dope that was taped around her chest,
and prayed that it didn't bulge out.

She saw Tasha sitting across from her, waiting for the same plane that she herself would
soon board. She didn't look too long though,

not wanting to make any contact with any of her girls until they landed safely and undetected in Florida. Mimi was scared, and it seemed like her senses were working overtime. She was aware of everything around her. Her heart was pounding and she couldn't stop her face from showing how nervous she was. *Just get through this. Please, God, just get us through this!*

Amra was in the restroom of the airport, her heart pounding. She was sick to her stomach, and she felt weak, as if she would pass out. She gripped the sink for support and turned on the cold water. She splashed the water onto her face and stared at her reflection. *We're not going to get away with this. It's too hot. This is way out of our league.* She looked at the gray sweatshirt and jeans that she had on and prayed that no one could tell that she had something taped to her chest. *Please let me get away with this.*

Amra walked out to the terminal and sat down in front of the boarding gate. She bit at her nails and tried to focus her mind on something else, but no matter how hard she tried, she couldn't stop thinking about getting caught.

Honey sat across from Mimi as if she had never seen her before. She wore a black business suit, and at her feet sat a black briefcase worth more than gold. *I wonder how much money*

Manolo is making from this lick. She tapped her foot against the ground. She looked at her watch and saw that it was almost time for them to board their plane.

Honey was shaken. She knew that if they got caught, they would do a lot of time, but she didn't intend on getting caught. She tried to keep her nervousness hidden, but she couldn't hide the butterflies floating around in her stomach.

She stood up and grabbed the briefcase when she heard them announce the boarding of their flight. With each step she took toward the gate, her nervousness grew. She felt her mouth getting dry and felt her stomach tie in knots when she made it to the security checkpoint. *Okay, make it through here, and I'm good.*

"Hi," an airline worker said. "Can you place your briefcase on the conveyor belt, please?"

Honey placed the briefcase on the belt and crossed her fingers. She had wrapped a towel around the dope. She prayed that it was the only thing they saw on the x-ray. She walked through the metal detector, and it didn't make a sound.

Another airline worker handed her the briefcase. "Thank you. Have a nice flight."

Honey had held her breath through the entire thing, and finally released a long sigh of relief. *Hell yeah!* She looked back at the line and winked at Amra as she stepped up next to be searched.

Amra stepped up and walked through with no problem. She continued walking to the plane.

Mimi, up next, stepped up and walked through with no problem. Even though she had gotten through, her heart was still racing. She didn't look back as Tasha stepped up.

Please let this be easy. Tasha could hear her heartbeat in her ears and she felt sick. She slowly walked through the detector, and her eyes grew wide when the alarm sounded loudly.

"Miss, please walk through again."

Tasha shook her head and walked through the metal detector a second time.

Beep! Beep! Beep!

"Do you have any metal objects on you?"

Tasha felt the lump in her throat. "No, I don't have anything."

The woman motioned for a male guard to come over. "Take her." She pointed to Tasha.

Tasha felt the tears forming behind her glasses as the security guard put his hand on the small of her back and escorted her into a small office. A tear slid down her cheek. The guard came over to her and ran a small device up and down her clothes. Tasha couldn't stop the tears from coming. The guard put the device to her face, and it beeped loudly. "It was your glasses," he said in a calm voice. "The metal frame made the detector go off."

Tasha looked at the guard and breathed deep. "Can I go now?"

"Yeah, you can go." He looked at her wiping tears from her face. "Are you okay to fly, Miss? You know you shouldn't be more than seven months pregnant when flying."

Tasha laughed to herself. "I'm fine. My ankles are just swollen and sore. They get to me sometimes." She walked out of the security room, and quickly boarded the plane and sat in her seat. She looked across the aisle at Honey and read her lips.

"What took you so long?"

"You don't want to know," Tasha whispered. She sat back and took five deep breaths. *Thank you, God!* She had never been so afraid in her life.

The planed landed in Florida at five P.M. The girls quickly exited the plane, and they all headed to the bathroom, where they all yelled at Tasha, "What the fuck took you so long to get on the plane?"

Tasha walked over to the sink and splashed water onto her face. "My glasses set off the metal detector. I thought I was caught." Tasha couldn't believe how lucky they had all been.

Honey looked in the mirror and fixed her hair. "Okay, let's go find Manolo's cousin."

They walked outside of the airport, and a tall darkskinned man with a huge gap in his teeth approached them. Honey led the way toward the man. The man didn't say anything to them. He just turned around, and they followed him to a black Escalade that sat near the curb. They got into the truck, and he drove off.

"Y'all look shook. It's cool. Y'all got the dope?"

Honey opened the briefcase she had carried through the airport and showed him the drugs. She asked, "You got the money?"

He nodded. "We'll make the trade at the hotel."

He drove them to the Marriott Hotel. When he got out of the car, he grabbed two briefcases from the back. Then he checked them in and led the way to their room.

As soon as they got into the room, Tasha started peeling the duct tape off her skin. "Damn! This shit hurts! I'm about to take off a nipple!"

Mimi slowly peeled the sticky tape off her chest.

The girls put the dope in a duffel bag that Manolo's cousin had sitting on the bed.

"Here's the money and the tickets. "Y'all know what to do next?"

"Yeah, we know what to do," Tasha replied.

Manolo's cousin didn't linger around to chat. He zipped the duffel bag full of drugs and quickly left the room.

As soon as he left, Amra ran over to the bed and opened the two briefcases full of money. "Damn!" she yelled, pulling stacks of money out.

Mimi went over to the bed and flipped through one of the stacks. "These are all hundreds!"

Honey looked at the suitcases and thought to herself,

It's got to be at least a couple hundred thousand in there.

Tasha got on the phone and called Manolo. As soon as he answered the phone, she said, "We got the money."

Manolo smiled to himself. "Good. See you tomorrow."

Tasha sat down in the chair. She looked around at the plush room they had for the night. "I am glad that this shit is done."

Mimi looked at her and busted out laughing. "Yeah, me too. But for real, Tasha, I was cracking up when your ass finally got on the plane. It looked like you was about to piss on yourself."

Amra and Honey started cracking up.

Tasha laughed. "I know I was looking crazy, because I was scared as hell. When they pulled me to the side, I started to dip out on they ass."

Her friends were laughing so hard, their eyes started to water.

Honey got serious again. "We ain't done yet. We still got to get this money back home."

The girls calmed down for the rest of the day. Tasha was busy thinking about Joe. She couldn't wait to get home to him. They all kept to themselves for the rest of the night, anticipating going back through the airport.

The next morning, they woke up and took a shuttle bus to the airport. They didn't have to dress up in ridiculous clothes, because taking money through the airport wasn't as hot as moving dope.

The girls sat together and waited for their flight. Honey had one of the suitcases, and Tasha had the other. Their flight didn't leave until nine o'clock, but they had arrived an hour early. All of them seemed to be more relaxed this time, knowing that it wasn't such a big risk.

The loud intercom sounded throughout the entire airport. "*Excuse me, passengers, the nine o'clock flight to Flint has been delayed. There is approximately a three-hour wait time. If you have any questions, please come to the front desk.*"

Amra shouted, "That's some bullshit! I'm not trying to wait here for three more hours!"

"It looks like we gon' be here for a while." Mimi layed down across the seats.

Amra smacked her lips then looked at Tasha. "Is there a different flight we could take?"

Tasha said, "Let's go check the flight listing."

Honey shrugged her shoulders and walked with Tasha. Tasha looked up at the flight schedule. "Nope. That was the only flight to Flint. We're just going to have to wait."

Honey studied the flight schedule, and a smirk spread across her face. "It's a flight leaving at nine, but it ain't headed to Flint."

Tasha looked back at the schedule to see what Honey was talking about. "The only other flight leaving at nine is for New York."

Honey said, "You thinking what I'm thinking?"

Tasha shook her head. She already knew what Honey was thinking. "I'm just trying to get this money back to Manolo so I can be done with this. I'm not trying to get into no more hot shit." She walked back and sat down, patiently waiting for their flight.

Three hours later, the girls boarded a plane home.

Tasha looked around at her friends, and instantly felt a knot in her stomach. She knew the stuff that they'd been doing was wrong, and prayed that their actions wouldn't catch up to them, that karma wouldn't come back to haunt her. *What goes around comes around,* she thought to herself.

Chapter Sixteen

"Bitch, you tried to rob me!" Keys screamed as he pinned Tasha up against his bedroom wall.

Tasha wanted to respond, wanted to lie and say she hadn't done it, but he was holding her neck so tight, she couldn't speak. She clawed at his hands, trying to get him to release her. She choked and gasped as Keys' fingers wrapped around her windpipe. "Stop!" she yelled between gasps. Her eyes felt like they were on fire, as if they would pop out of her head.

Keys banged her hard against the wall, and she felt her neck snap repeatedly as he shook her. "Bitch, you tried to rob me?"

Tasha could feel her lungs sizzle as she struggled to breathe in air. Keys was killing her, choking the life out of her, and no matter how much she struggled, she couldn't stop him.

Her eyes searched the room for something she could defend herself with, but there was nothing. She heard footsteps run into the room, and she watched as someone swung a metal candle-holder hard against Keys' head. Keys let go of Tasha's neck, and she fell to the floor gasping for air. Then he fell next to her and stared at her as blood drained from his head onto the carpet. Tasha stared in bewilderment as she watched him die.

She sat up to see who had come to her rescue, and she looked into her own eyes and saw herself holding the candleholder, blood all over her hands.

Tasha woke up sweating, screaming, "No, I didn't do this! I didn't do this!" She looked at the clock that sat next to her bed. It said 3:00 A.M. She rubbed her neck, remembering how Keys had choked her in her dream. She breathed in deeply and got up and walked to the bathroom. She looked in the mirror and started to cry.

"I'm sorry," she said to herself as she sat down on the toilet. Something inside of her was making her weak. Ever since they had killed Keys, her conscience had been fucking with her. *I just want to go home. I want to be with Joe.* She remembered how safe she felt in his arms.

She heard someone knock on the door and quickly wiped her eyes before opening the door.

Mimi looked at Tasha. "Hey. Are you all right?"

"Yeah, I'm good. I'll talk to you in the morning."

Mimi shook her head and walked past Tasha into the bathroom.

The next morning, Tasha woke up to the ringing of her cell phone. She looked at the caller ID, and cut off Manolo's call. *I'm not fucking with Manolo any more. We gave him his money. He needs to stop calling.* Tasha sat up in bed as Amra walked into the room.

"Hey, Tasha," she said, walking over to her dresser.

"Hey, has Manolo been calling you?" Tasha asked.

"Yeah, he been calling, but I haven't answered the phone. I ain't fucking with him like that no more. Besides, I can find my own niggas to hustle. I don't need him pimping me."

Tasha frowned at the word "pimping". She'd never thought about it like that, but that was in fact what Manolo had been doing. She felt even more disgusted with herself.

The day went by slowly for Tasha. She and her friends were all chilling together. It had been a long time since they had just hung out and not talked about what group of dudes they were trying to hustle.

"I think I might go back home," Tasha said. "I don't know. I just think I need to be there. After that shit with Keys, I'm not really feeling Flint like that."

Mimi pulled her candy jar from underneath her bed. "Why are you tripping? It's over with. It's been almost a month, and ain't nobody said shit about it since then. The police don't know who did it. They probably think he was killed over some drug beef or something."

Honey added, "Yeah, Tasha, you got to calm down. If that's why you want to go back to the D, then you're worrying for nothing."

Tasha watched Mimi roll up a blunt and begin to smoke it. Tasha had her reasons for wanting to go back home. She didn't feel right about what she'd done to Keys. *These bitches acting like that shit is cool, like we in the clear just because they haven't heard anything about it.*

"Let's go out tonight," Amra said. "I'm tired of sitting in the house stressing over whether we going to get caught or not."

Honey jumped up. "I got the bathroom first." She ran out of the room and into the bathroom before anyone could protest.

Tasha got up and walked into the bedroom. She locked the door behind her so Amra wouldn't come in and interrupt her. She reached underneath her bed and pulled out a shoebox that she kept her money in. She opened it and pulled out the money she had managed to save since coming to Flint. When she was done counting, she thought, *Fifteen grand . . . enough to get me back to New York and have me on my feet for at least a couple months.*

Tasha was already making plans to go back home. No matter what her girls said, she knew it was only a matter of time before all the shit they'd been doing came back around to bite them in the ass. She put the money back in the box and put it under her bed, then picked up her cell phone and dialed the number to the hospital where Ms. Pat was being treated.

"Grace Sinai, Cancer Ward," a friendly voice said. "How can I help you?"

"Hi. Can you connect me to Patricia Rodgers' room?"

The receptionist connected her, and Ms. Pat answered the phone. "Hello?"

Tasha was bothered at the fact that she sounded so weak. "Hi, Ms. Pat. It's Tasha. How are you feeling?"

Ms. Pat slowly responded, "I'm fine. The doctors say the surgery went well."

Tasha could hear the pain in Ms. Pat's voice. "That's good. I told you everything would be okay," she said, trying to sound optimistic. She knew Ms. Pat was in a lot of pain right now, and she was just trying to be supportive. "I just wanted to let you know that I love you."

Just then, Amra knocked on the bedroom door, and Tasha got up and opened it. "I'm going to let you talk to Amra now, but after that, I want you to get as much rest as you can." She handed Amra the phone, and then walked out of the room, to give her some privacy.

Tasha waited for Amra to get off the phone before she went back into the room. Amra was sitting on the bed with a worried look on her face when Tasha re-entered the room.

"Are you okay?" Tasha asked her.

Amra shook her head from left to right. "She doesn't sound good."

Tasha quickly replied, "She just had surgery. It's going to take her some time to regain her strength. That's it. She'll be fine." Tasha didn't want Amra to worry about her mother.

"Let's get dressed before Honey and Mimi leave us."

Tasha put on a silver spaghetti strap Dolce & Gabbana top and black jeans that folded at the bottom, and silver Manolo Blahnik shoes that strapped at the back of her ankles. She looked in the mirror and put on her Tiffany jewelry, and then applied her makeup. By the time she was finished getting dressed, all of her friends were sitting on her bed waiting.

Honey wore an earth green Dior dress, Amra had on pink Roberto Cavalli pants with a white bra top, and Mimi was wearing a brown-and-cream chinchilla jacket and tight Prada jeans.

When the girls arrived at the club, there was a line around the block. They never waited in line though. Tasha walked up to the front of the line. The bouncer was so busy looking at her ass that he didn't charge her or her girls to get into the club.

Tasha led the way through the crowded club and found a table. Mimi immediately took off the chinchilla jacket and made her way out onto the dance floor. Tasha watched as dudes immediately turned their heads when Mimi walked past them. She started to laugh because she knew Mimi was enjoying every bit of the attention. Amra got up and joined Mimi in the middle of a circle of dudes who were watching them dance. Tasha was chilling, enjoying the hip-hop music that vibrated through the club.

"You want a drink?" Honey asked.

Tasha looked toward the bar and saw that it wasn't that crowded. She got up and followed Honey to the bar. Men's heads turned when

Honey and Tasha walked past them. They were showstoppers, and the other girls in the club quickly grew jealous.

Tasha sat down at the bar. Before she got a chance to order a drink, a good looking brown-skinned brother sat next to her. "Can I buy you a drink?" She looked at the man with cornrows sitting next to her and smiled. "Sure, an iced tea," she replied.

The man ordered her a Long Island iced tea.

Honey tapped on Tasha's shoulder and whispered in her ear, "I'm going to the bathroom."

Tasha stood up and offered her hand to the man that bought her drink. "Tasha," she said, introducing herself.

The man looked her in her eyes, intrigued by her beauty. He shook her hand softly. "Troy."

"Thanks for the drink." Tasha got up and began to follow Honey to the bathroom. When the girls went into the bathroom, Honey said, "Damn, girl! Who was that? He is fine."

Tasha laughed and waved her hand in dismissal. "He's all right." She wiped the sweat from her neckline and waited for Honey to come out of the stall. Honey touched up her makeup, and they went back to their table.

Tasha saw that the dance floor was packed, so she got up and joined Amra and Mimi on the floor. She danced sexily, shaking her ass to the Southern beats of T-Pain. "Buy U a Drank" was blaring throughout the club. She knew she had an audience, and was fine with that as long as they looked but didn't touch.

Tasha looked over at Amra and noticed that she was stumbling. *Damn! She's drunk already*.

It was hot in the club, and Amra was sweating. A dude picked her up, and she straddled him and started grinding on the dance floor. They were practically fucking on the dance floor. Tasha could tell that Amra wasn't in her right mind. The dude started feeling on Amra's body. He untied the bra top she had on and began feeling on her bare breasts.

Tasha marched over to her friend and pulled her away from the guy. "What are you doing? Amra, let's go."

The dude grabbed Amra's arm and pushed Tasha out of his way.

"Don't fucking touch me!" Tasha yelled as she snatched Amra's arm away from him. "You better get the fuck back! What you think, I'm about to let you just take advantage of my girl? You need to find another ho, 'cuz it ain't happening over here." Tasha got in the guy's face.

Honey saw the scene and quickly made her way over to Tasha's side.

The man mumbled, "Bitch!"

Honey stepped up. "Who the fuck do you think you talking to?"

The man waved his hand when he noticed that he was causing a scene, and then walked away.

Amra could barely stand on her own, and Tasha had her arm around her, holding her up.

"What the fuck is wrong with her?" Honey asked.

Tasha looked at Amra. "What did you drink?"

"Nothing. I haven't had anything to drink."

Tasha looked at Honey in confusion.

"Come on," Honey said, leading the way to the bathroom. The air in there was cooler than the musty, humid air on the dance floor.

As Amra went in, she immediately collapsed over the toilet, throwing up.

"Mimi, what did she drink?" Tasha yelled.

Mimi shook her head. "I didn't see her drink nothing, unless it was from somebody else's cup. We've been dancing since we got here. Shit, I'm not ready to go yet, so I hope she feels better when she's done hurling."

Tasha walked into the stall and rubbed Amra's back as she threw up into the toilet. "She needs to go home. I'll go with her. B, you stay here with Mimi."

Honey agreed, because she really didn't want to leave anyway. "Call me on my cell when you make it home," she told Tasha.

Tasha nodded her head and helped Amra up. She wet a paper towel and wiped some of the sweat off Amra's body. "Come on, sweetie." Tasha let Amra lean on her.

Tasha walked out of the bathroom with Amra, and guided her through the crowded club. The air outside felt good against her skin. "You feel better?" she asked Amra.

Amra shook her head no, and Tasha sat her down against the building. She went to the curb of the street and hailed a cab. She opened the door and said, "Can you help me put my friend in the cab?"

The driver got out and put Amra into the back seat. Just as Tasha was getting ready to get in, a man got out of a car that was sitting across the street from the club and yelled, "Excuse me!"

Tasha turned and saw that it was the man she had met earlier at the bar.

"Hey!" he called out to her again.

Tasha turned around. "I don't really have time to talk right now."

Troy replied, "You better make time, shorty."

Tasha turned around and smacked her lips. "Excuse me?"

Troy pulled out his police badge and walked close up on her and put his face by her right ear. "I'm a detective for the Flint Police Department. I know about what you did to Keys."

Tasha's heart dropped, and her breath became shallow. Lightheaded, she thought she would choke on her words if she said anything. She closed her eyes, trying to stop the tears from coming. "I don't know what you're talking about." Tasha got into the cab, and Troy put his hand on the door to stop her from closing it.

"I think you do. I was there. I saw everything." Tasha tapped the driver. "Let's go."

The driver waited for Troy to close the back door. Troy touched Tasha's face and made her look him in the eye. "Meet me here tomorrow at two o'clock. Don't be late." He handed her a card with his number on it, and closed the cab door.

When the driver pulled off, Tasha began to cry. She looked over at Amra, who was passed out in the seat. *What am I going to do? He knows. He saw us.* Tasha knew she was going down for Keys' murder. "Fuck! *Fuck!*" she yelled, hitting the seat of the cab. Her heart was pumping and her mind was racing. She was scared, and her head was aching from thinking so hard.

When the cab arrived at Tammy's house, she woke Amra up and helped her into the house.

They walked into their room, and Tasha laid Amra in her bed. Tasha didn't want to tell Amra about Troy Smith. She'd seen how Amra reacted after she had killed Keys, so she decided to only tell Honey. She tucked Amra into her bed and noticed that she looked pale. Her eyes were dark around the lids. She knew Amra was sick. *I'm going to let her sleep it off.*

Tasha picked up her cell phone and called Honey. She knew she wouldn't hear her phone ring because the club played loud music and was very noisy, but she left a message. "Honey, it's me," she said, her voice shaking. She couldn't seem to calm herself down. "You need to come home quick. Somebody knows. Call me as soon as you get this message." *I knew this was coming. I knew something wasn't right.*

Troy looked at the picture of the woman he had confronted that night. "Tasha," he said to himself. He admired the picture. She was beautiful. He couldn't believe she had gotten caught up in a murder. He went into the kitchen and pulled out a pint of Rémy and drank it straight from the bottle. He could have easily arrested Tasha on the evidence that he already had, but he was after the big fish. He wanted Jamaica, and he knew that if Tasha had gotten Keys to trust her, then she could do the same with Jamaica. *She's*

*either going to help me get him, or I'm going to
get her. Twenty-five years to life . . . she'll see
things my way.*

Honey walked into the house alone at three in
the morning. Mimi had left the club with some
dude. She made her way to her room, where Tasha was pacing back and forth, waiting for her.
Honey could tell that she'd been crying. "Tasha,
what's up? What's wrong?"

Tasha stopped pacing. "He knows, Honey, he
knows. He told me."

Tasha was shaking, and Honey didn't know
what she was talking about. "Who is *he*? And
what does *he* know?"

"The guy from the bar. He was a cop, Honey.
He knows we killed Keys. I told you. You told me
to stop tripping, but I told you that somebody
was going to find out. We should have gone back
to New York."

Honey's eyes shot open. "A cop?" she asked,
almost yelling. "What did he say to you? Did you
tell him anything?"

Tasha yelled back, "Do you think I'm stupid? I
didn't tell him shit. He just knows. He told me to
meet him in front of the club tomorrow."

Honey sat down on her bed. She shook her
head. "He doesn't know shit!"

"He said he saw us, Honey."

Honey walked over to Tasha and grabbed her shoulders. "Tasha, think! If he knew something, he would have arrested you right then and there. He's bluffing. He doesn't know shit. He wants something."

Tasha tried to calm herself down, but she couldn't. *She's so calm, but she ain't the one he came up to.* "What do we do?"

"The only thing we can do. Give him what he wants. You have to meet him tomorrow."

Tasha shook her head. "No, I'm not doing it. Why can't you go? Why can't Mimi go? Hell! Amra can even go."

"He told *you*. *You* have to go."

Tasha knew that Honey was right. She had to find out what the detective wanted. *It's all going to fall back on me. I have to fix this. If I don't, I'm going to go down for all this shit.*

Honey knew what Tasha was thinking just from the look in her eyes. She walked over to her friend and hugged her tight. "Tasha, we are in this together, okay? I'm not going to let anything happen to you."

"Don't tell Amra about this," Tasha said. "I don't want her worrying about this right now."

"Mimi doesn't need to know either."

Tasha then got into her bed and fell into a restless sleep.

***

When Tasha woke up the next morning, she felt exhausted. She had tossed and turned all night, and the thought of her getting caught for Keys' murder made it impossible to go to sleep. She looked at the clock. It was ten o'clock. She thought about the money that she had saved underneath her bed, and she instantly wanted to go home. She knew she couldn't though. *I need to handle this.*

Amra came in and saw her deep in thought.

"Are you feeling better?" Tasha asked.

"No, I feel like shit. I don't know what happened. One minute I was fine, and the next I felt like I was going to die."

Tasha laughed. "I thought you were drunk."

Amra plopped down on the bed. "Nah, I didn't even drink last night. I think it was just way too hot in there. I fucked my leg up last night, though." She lifted up her pajama pants and showed Tasha the sore on her leg.

Tasha frowned. "Damn! You fucked your shit up. It probably happened when you fell on the floor in the bathroom at the club. That's why it's all bruised up around it. You need to put something on that."

While Amra went to get a bandage, Tasha thought about telling her about Troy Smith, but she knew her friend would panic. *I don't have time to be worried about her right now. I just need to get us out of this.*

Tasha stayed in bed just thinking. She desperately wanted to be with Joe, but the way her life was going, it didn't seem like she would ever make it back to him.

She got out of bed and threw on some Enyce jeans and a red-and-white Enyce shirt. She pulled her hair back in a neat ponytail. She looked into the mirror and could tell that she hadn't gotten any sleep the night before.

Honey walked into the room and said, "Don't worry, he doesn't know anything."

Tasha was hoping Troy wouldn't show up. She was shaking nervously, tapping her foot during the cab ride. She got out and walked toward the club, her heart beating like a drum as she got closer and closer to her destination. She saw a black Lexus sitting in the empty parking lot of the club. She heard the car horn and saw him roll down the window. She recognized his face and started walking toward him.

He hit the unlock button, and Tasha got into the car. "I'm glad you made it," he said.

Tasha rolled her eyes. "Stop with the bullshit. What do you know?"

Troy smiled at her smart mouth. He tossed a folder into her lap. "That's what I know."

Tasha quickly opened the folder and flipped through the pictures inside. She saw pictures of her with Keys, and more importantly, pictures of her and her friends entering and exiting Keys' house, and of her with the pillowcase in her hand that they'd used to carry the money in the night of his murder. Tasha's heart stopped, and she tried not to show she was scared. *If he wanted to, he could arrest me off of this, so what does he want?* "Why are you showing me this? What do you want?"

Troy heard the quiver in her voice and knew she was scared. He looked at the beautiful young woman who sat next to him. "I want you to work for me. You see, I could easily put you and your little friends away for a long time, but that's not what I'm here for. As far as I'm concerned, that's one less scum off the street. You scratch my back, I'll scratch yours."

"What do you mean?"

"I can make this disappear, but only if you help me."

"What do I have to do?"

"There's a new face in town. In the streets he's known as Jamaica, and he's moving heavy weight. I want you to do the same thing you did to Keys. I want you to get in close and get me the information I need to put his ass behind bars. After that, you're free. I'll keep my end of the bargain . . . if you keep yours."

Tasha was in no position to refuse the offer. "How do I know this is going to be a one-time thing?"

Troy laughed. "My word is bond. Give me a number where I can reach you at."

Tasha took a deep breath and reluctantly gave him her cell phone number.

Troy smiled. "Be expecting my call, shorty."

Tasha shook her head and quickly got out of the car. *I hate this shit. I didn't do this by myself, but I have to fix it by myself. I'm tired of niggas holding shit over my head. I don't even know if I can trust him. I don't know shit about him.* Tasha knew it wouldn't be hard for her to charm the man Troy was going to put her on. She just hated that she didn't have a choice. Troy had quickly taken the place of Manolo in her life, but in his hustle, the stakes were higher.

As soon as Tasha walked in the door, Honey was waiting for her. "What happened?" she whispered, trying to make sure Mimi and Amra didn't hear.

"You were wrong. He does know. He has the pictures to prove it too."

Honey's heart dropped when she heard the news. She looked at Tasha in despair. "What now? What happens next?"

Tasha lowered her head. "I have to help him arrest some drug dealer that's been taking over since Keys died. He says if I help him, he will make Keys' murder disappear."

"And if you don't?"

"We'll all go down for the murder."

"How does he expect you to do that?"

"How else? He wants me to do the same thing I did with Keys."

"That shouldn't be that hard. You had that nigga whipped after the first date."

"This is different. It's not a game."

Jamaica and his right-hand man, Tariq, sat in his hotel room, counting the money they'd just made. Jamaica stopped counting and looked over at Tariq. "We could never make this money this fast back home. Flint is where it's at, duke."

Tariq smiled and continued to count the piles of money on the bed. Without taking his eyes off the money, he replied, "We did it, son. We're big time now. That new shit you brought back got the streets in a frenzy. I told you when you came here we were going to make major moves."

Jamaica pulled his gun off his waistline and set it on the bed. He then stood up and walked toward the window and opened the blinds. He walked out onto the balcony and looked at the city lights. He took a deep breath of Flint's fresh air. *If money keeps rolling in like this, I might not go back home. I can't believe how our dope is driving niggas nuts here. I don't want too much attention, though. I ain't trying to get knocked.*

Tariq stuck half of his body onto the balcony. "Wanna hit this?" He offered Jamaica the blunt he had in his hand.

"Nah, duke, I'm good. I want to stay focused."

Tariq looked at Jamaica like he was crazy. "I feel you, but me, I got to stay high."

Tariq went back into the hotel room and continued to smoke, while Jamaica stayed out on the balcony, thinking about how good life was at the moment.

Troy had Tasha right where he wanted her. She knows she doesn't have a choice. He knew that Jamaica would not be able to resist her. She was what every nigga wanted.

Troy pulled his holster off his waistline and set it on his living room table. He felt bad about blackmailing Tasha, but she was the only way he could get something on Jamaica. Keys was very careful when he was alive, and if she was able to get him to trust her, then she had to be good.

He picked up his case files, opened them and looked at the pictures he had taken of Tasha. He didn't want to waste any time; he wanted her to get on Jamaica as soon as possible. One of his little niggas from around the way had told him where Jamaica liked to hang out, and he planned on sending Tasha there the next night.

He pulled Tasha's number out of his wallet and smiled to himself. With her working for him, he was so much closer to getting the bad guy.

Chapter Seventeen

Tasha received a call from Troy the following morning, telling her that Jamaica would be at Junior's that night. "You need to be there tonight," he told her. "I need you to get in good with him quick. He usually stops in around eight o'clock. I'll be there watching you, so don't fuck up."

"How will I know what he looks like?"

"You'll know when you see him. He'll be the nigga who comes in with a group of dudes. He's the ringleader though. He runs it all. It's not hard to spot him."

Tasha hung up her cell phone without saying goodbye. *Damn! What did I get myself into? How do I know this is going to be the last time this nigga tries to use me? Or, how do I know he's not going to arrest me after he gets what he wants?*

Tasha walked into Mimi's room. She saw her asleep in her bed, and Amra's bed was neatly made up with a note on the top of the blanket. Tasha walked over to the bed and picked up the letter. It read: *Went out for a minute. Be back in a few. Amra.*

Tasha threw the letter on the bed and whispered, "I wonder where she went." She shrugged her shoulders and walked out of the room and thought about her task at hand for later that night.

As Amra sat in the doctor's office waiting for her name to be called, she flipped through a magazine. She thought to herself, *I wish they would hurry up. Please, God, don't let me be pregnant. I do not need this right now.* She hadn't been feeling well lately, and was always fatigued. If she was pregnant, she had no idea who the baby's daddy was. Most of her sexual encounters happened when she was either drunk or high. And she had engaged in sex with so many men, even she had lost count.

The nurse stuck her head out of the door that led to the back. "Amra Rodgers."

Amra took a deep breath and whispered, "Here goes nothing!" and then proceeded to the door where the nurse was waiting for her.

The nurse escorted Amra into a small room and told her, "Wait here. Dr. Katz will be with you shortly."

Amra began to feel butterflies in her stomach as she sat there waiting for the doctor to enter the room. She'd been there a week before to get a checkup and wasn't this nervous. She had a gut feeling she was pregnant. The nausea became unbearable, and she felt the contents of her stomach threatening to erupt as her body temperature began to rise. *I got to go home and lay down.*

Dr. Katz walked in fifteen minutes later. "Good morning, Amra. Good to see you again.

Amra mustered up a smile. "Hey, Dr. Katz."

Dr. Katz grew a concerned look on his face and said in a soft voice, "The receptionist has been calling you all week. We needed you to come in."

Amra's heart dropped. She already knew. She dropped her head and whispered, "I'm pregnant." She placed her hand over her stomach and imagined it big, with stretch marks all over. A tear formed in her eye as she looked at the doctor. "I'm not trying to have a baby right now. I can't have a baby right now. I-I want an abortion."

Dr. Katz took a seat on the stool closest to Amra. "I think it's a little more serious than that. Your blood test came back positive. Amra, you're HIV-positive, and it's progressing quickly into full-blown AIDS."

"*What?* What the fuck you mean? That test can't be right!"

"With new technology, infected people can prolong their—"

Amra stormed out of the office before he could even finish his sentence. She was in a state of shock the whole ride home. The tears stopped, and she seemed to be in a zombie-like trance. She didn't even get off at her stop. She couldn't focus on anything. She regretted all the nights of unprotected sex. *I'm dead! I don't even know where it came from . . . I mean, who it came from. My life is over!*

"You ready?" Troy asked.

Tasha, sitting in the passenger seat of his car, shook her head up and down. "Yeah, I'm ready . . . ready for this to be over!" she said sarcastically.

Troy quickly responded, "You have a long while before this shit is over. Get the job done."

Tasha smacked her lips and folded her arms tightly against her chest.

"Don't fuck with me, shorty. If I suspect any bullshit on your part, you know where you'll be headed."

As they sat in the parking lot of Junior's, Tasha grew more and more frustrated with her situation. The tension was so thick, you could cut it with a knife. "What are we waiting for?" she asked in a smart way. Troy kept his eyes on the building and didn't respond to her, so she rolled her eyes and started to look out of her window at the pedestrians and the traffic jam in the streets.

"Showtime!" Troy said as he saw Jamaica and his crew enter Junior's.

Tasha tried to get a glance at the infamous Jamaica, but by the time she looked up, the men were entering the building, and all she could see was the back of their heads.

"Jamaica is the cat with the blue NY hat and the platinum chain around his neck. That's the man you're after. I want you to get acquainted. Okay, go on."

Tasha took a deep breath. As she got out of the car, Troy said, "And don't slam my door!"

Tasha smiled to herself. She cocked the car door back and slammed it as hard as she could. *That felt good,* she thought as she headed toward the front entrance.

Troy shook his head and watched as she walked toward the entrance. *Damn!* he thought, admiring Tasha's sandy-brown hair that matched her skin. He licked his lips as he watched her ass and Coke bottle shape.

Tasha entered the building, and as she walked to an open table, all of the guys she passed stared at her beauty.

"Damn!"

"Hey, ma!"

Tasha ignored them. She was used to that type of reaction from men, but today she was on a mission. She sat down at an empty table and began to look for her target. She noticed that the groups of guys across from her were the fellas she had seen entering the building. She made eye contact with one of them. He was very dark, with perfect white teeth and had deep waves on top of his head, which appealed to Tasha. But he wasn't wearing a platinum chain. She quickly glanced at the other men and noticed that none of them was wearing a platinum chain.

The dark-skinned man that Tasha had been scoping out got up and walked toward her. "Hey, ma. Can I sit?"

Tasha wanted to say yeah so badly. Any other day she would have been on him, but today wasn't the day. "I'm waiting for someone."

He sat down anyway and smiled slyly. "Whoever you're waiting for is a damn fool. He got you waiting here all by yourself. If that was me, I would have been waiting on *you*."

Tasha smiled, but she wasn't interested. *This nigga needs to move so that I can find Jamaica.*

"What's yo' name?"

"Tasha. What's yours?"

The dude sat back in the booth and seemed to relax before he replied, "Tariq."

Damn! Wrong nigga, she thought to herself. Just as she was about to dismiss his ass, a man walked past them and sat at the same table that Tariq had come from. Tasha noticed the chain on his neck. "Bingo!" she whispered as she got a glimpse of Jamaica's backside.

"What you say?"

"Yo', who is that?"

Tariq turned around. "Who? Him? That's my man, Jamaica."

Tasha smiled and looked at the back of Jamaica's head. "Tariq—it was Tariq, right?—tell Jamaica I would like to talk to him."

Tariq got a salty look on his face and looked back, "Oh . . . okay," he said as he slowly rose up from the table. *That bitch got some nerve,* he thought as he walked back to his table with a bruised ego. He whispered something in Jamaica's ear, and then looked back at Tasha. Jamaica didn't even turn around to look at her. He just shook his head and continued to eat his cheesecake.

Tasha was insulted. *Who this nigga think he is? He didn't even look at me.* At that moment, the waiter walked over to Tasha and asked her for her order. "A burger and fries," she said, never taking her eyes off the man they called Jamaica.

As Tasha waited for her food, she saw Troy walk in. He walked past her and sat at the counter and signaled for a waitress. He spun his chair slightly around to position himself toward her, and shot a look to let her know she needed to get on her job. She nodded her head to let him know she was on task.

Jamaica stood up and began to turn around. Tasha thought, *Okay, Jamaica, let's see if your looks are as big as your reputation.* As Jamaica turned around, Tasha squinted her eyes in disbelief, and couldn't believe what she saw. "Oh my God! Joe?" she yelled out in a state of shock.

Joe looked in her direction. "Tasha?" He walked over to her with his arms out and gave her a hug.

Tasha felt good in his arms and took a deep breath. Joe held her tight and rubbed her back as he embraced her. Tasha was speechless. She glanced over at Troy, who was watching her closely. "What are you doing here?" she asked, their hands intertwined.

"I'm here with my people. I needed a little vacation, and I'm here for a while."

Tasha didn't know what to say. "Oh!"

Troy smirked, knowing half of the battle was already won. *Hell yeah! She already knows this nigga. This should be like taking candy from a baby. He already trusts her.* Troy watched closely as they talked to each other. He couldn't make out what they were saying, so eventually he stopped trying to. He had seen all he needed to see. He pulled out his wallet, threw some money on the table, and walked out.

Joe joined Tasha at her table, and his friends sat behind them in their own booth. "How have you been?" he asked her.

Tasha had to take deep breaths to stop the tears from coming. She wanted to tell him everything, but she couldn't. *I can't set you up,* she thought to herself. She could either be loyal to herself and her friends and fix their mess by doing what Troy wanted her to do, or she could be loyal to Joe and not go through with the setup.

"You all right?"

Tasha snapped out of her daze. "Yeah, I'm okay. I missed you so much."

Joe didn't reply. He just gave her a sexy smile that she knew meant, "I missed you too."

Tariq came over to the table and whispered into Jamaica's ear.

Jamaica told Tasha, "Look, I got to go handle some business right now."

Tasha's heart almost broke in pieces. *I don't want you to go.*

"Do you think it's possible for us to get together tonight?"

Tasha felt a sharp pain vibrate in her heart. *I can't do this. I love him too much. I have to tell him about Troy.* "Joe . . .

I . . ." She pictured Troy putting handcuffs on her and taking her to jail. "I'll call you when I'm ready."

Joe leaned over and kissed her on the cheek softly. "Tasha, I'm glad we ran into each other. I wasn't going to call you until I finished handling all my business, but I'm happy to see you. I'll see you tonight." He put his hand on Tasha's face.

Tasha smiled. "See you then."

Joe got up, and his crew followed him out of the door.

Tasha was devastated. She buried her head in her arms. *What the fuck! What are the odds that my target would be Joe? He is supposed to be in New York. It wasn't supposed to happen like this. I can't do this to him.*

Tasha got up and stormed out of the restaurant. Troy was waiting for her by his car with a smug look on his face. "I'm not doing this!" she said as she walked past him.

Troy walked behind her. "Then you might as well get ready to spend the rest of your life in prison."

Tasha continued to walk away from him. "Do what you got to do then. I can't do that to him! I won't!" she yelled at Troy. She was tired of being blackmailed, and she didn't want to set up the one man in her life who loved her and treated her right.

"You don't have a choice! Tasha, you can either save your own ass, or save his. It's up to you. Don't be stupid. Would he do the same thing for you? That nigga got bitches like you all over town. You ain't nothing special. Don't let love land your ass behind bars." Troy could see that his words were getting to her. To make sure that she saw things his way, he picked up his cell phone and called his lieutenant. "Hey, lieutenant, this is Smith. I need you to send out a car to pick up these ladies for me. They are suspects in—"

Tasha walked over to Troy and snatched his phone from his hand. She hung up on the lieutenant and said, "Fuck you, Troy!"

Troy watched as she pulled at her hair and walked in a circle, trying to figure out what she should do. She approached him aggressively and said, "I'll do it!"

Troy smiled. "I thought so. Now, get in the car so I can take you home."

Tasha glared at him. "No, thanks. I'll walk!"

Amra looked in the mirror, and for the first time, she saw the signs of the disease all in her face. *How did I do this to myself?* she asked herself. *How stupid can I be? I've been having sex with so many different men. I never thought this would happen to me. I wish I could just take it all back.*

Amra felt empty inside. While she was struggling to save her mother's life, she had been willingly killing herself slowly over time. *I don't even know who gave it to me,* she thought as she stared at her reflection in despair. *Why did this happen to me?* She tried to retrace her steps to find out where the disease had come from, but didn't know where to start. She was promiscuous before she came to Flint, and didn't know if she had just caught it, or if she had been passing it along for years. She'd never even thought to ask men to use a condom, knowing that once they got a taste of her loving, it would be her payday. *I'm paying all right. I'm dying!*

Amra was so lost and confused. It didn't make sense to her. *How can I have AIDS?* She gripped the sink and slumped slowly onto the floor and curled up tightly in a ball. She closed her eyes and prayed that she would wake up and it would all be a bad dream. "Please, God, help me!" she pleaded as she rocked back and forth. She didn't understand why this was happening to her.

Amra didn't want anyone to know. She thought about what people would think about her. *I can't tell anybody, not even Tasha.* She was feeling so many different things; she was embarrassed, afraid of dying, and in a state of shock. Catching AIDS never crossed her mind. It always seemed like something that she heard about but never encountered. But now the reality was hitting home. Now she was the one infected with the deadly disease, and it was killing her that she could have prevented it.

Tasha walked into the house, crying hard. She was confused and afraid, but most of all, she didn't want to be the one to help nab Joe. *I didn't even know he was dealing drugs like that. I mean, I knew he had money, I just never thought he was in the game this big.*

Tasha saw Mimi and Tammy in the living room watching TV. She walked past them without saying anything and headed straight to Honey's room.

Honey was doing her hair when Tasha walked in. she could see Tasha's reflection in the mirror and immediately saw her red eyes and pale skin. "What happened?" She turned around to face her friend.

"Joe . . . it's Joe," Tasha started. "Troy wants me to help him arrest Joe. I saw him today. They call him 'Jamaica' in Flint."

Honey's mouth dropped to the floor, and her mind began to race. *I can't believe this shit! Tasha better not try to fuck us over to save him. She has to do this.* "What are you going to do?"

Tasha shrugged her shoulders. "I don't know. I don't think I can do this, especially not to him."

"You have to do this. It's not a choice. You have to think about everybody in the situation, Tasha. If it was me or Amra or Mimi, we would do it, but for some reason the cop chose you, so you got to do this. You have to get Keys' murder to disappear."

Tasha knew what she had to do and didn't need Honey drumming it into her head. "I know!" she yelled.

Honey watched her leave the room. *She better stop tripping.* Honey wasn't trying to go to jail because Tasha couldn't bring herself to go against her boyfriend. She wasn't having that at all. *The only reason we even robbed Keys was to get them that damn money for Ms. Pat. So she needs to remember that shit and handle this.*

Tasha made her way to her room and sat down and thought about Joe. She wanted to warn him. She wanted to tell him about Troy blackmailing her, but she knew that he would not be able to get her out of this. *I helped kill a man, and now I have to turn Joe in to cover it up.* She decided to lie down and take a nap before she went out that night with Joe. *Maybe I'll wake up with a clearer head.*

Amra entered the room and was glad to see that Tasha was asleep. She didn't feel like talking to anyone. She just wanted to be left alone, to deal with her own problems without hearing about anybody else's. She walked over to her bed and picked up her cell phone. She dialed her mother's number and waited anxiously as the phone rang.

"Hello?" Ms. Pat answered.

Amra smiled at the sound of her mother's voice. It felt good to hear it. She instantly wished she'd called more often. "Hi, Ma," Amra said in between sobs, as her tears began to flow again.

Ms. Pat knew her daughter like the back of her hand, and could tell that something was bothering her. "What's wrong, baby?"

"Nothing. I just miss talking to you. I miss home." Amra had already decided not to tell her mother that she'd contracted the deadly virus. She talked to her mother for a couple hours, saying all the things she normally wouldn't say. She wanted her mother to know exactly how she felt about her.

Ms. Pat could tell that something was wrong. She just didn't know exactly what it was.

"I love you, Ma," Amra said. It was something she had avoided saying for a long time. *I do love you, Momma,* she thought as she listened to her mother talk on the other end of the phone.

Amra talked to her mother for more than three hours that day. She told her mother everything that she had neglected to say over the years. She wanted to make sure that her mother knew that she appreciated her. They had experienced their share of arguments and differences, but Ms. Pat had never failed to be there for her daughter. Now that Amra knew she was dying, she wanted to be close to the woman who had brought her into the world. *It's something I should have done a long time ago.* She regretted all the times she had taken her mother for granted.

Amra hung up the phone and crawled underneath her covers. Exhausted, she just wanted to lie down and relax for a while. She looked at Tasha sleeping soundly in her bed, and wished she had listened to her when she had tried to tell her to calm down. *You were right. I should have been smart. All the niggas I've had sex with weren't worth my life.*

Chapter Eighteen

Tasha woke up from her nap and looked at the clock that sat on the nightstand that stood between her and Amra's bed. It was only six in the evening, so she had a lot of time before she called Joe. She looked over at Amra, who was lying on her stomach and writing in a diary. Tasha stood up and stretched her arms. "When did you start keeping a journal?"

Amra shrugged her shoulders. "I don't know. Right now, I have too many thoughts to keep them all in my head."

Tasha could see there was something bothering her. "Are you all right?" she asked, genuinely concerned.

"Yeah, I'm good," Amra whispered.

Tasha knew she was lying, but she had too many problems of her own to be worried about Amra's. Amra wanted to tell Tasha about her disease, but she didn't want anyone feeling sorry for her. *I don't need sympathy right now. I don't know what I need, but I know I don't need people turning their noses up at me, judging me.* Amra didn't know how she was supposed to feel. *What am I supposed to say? I'm dying, and there is nothing I can do about it?* She tried not to think about it and was trying to live a normal life, but she looked at stuff differently now that her days on this earth were numbered.

Every single thought that popped into her mind was followed by the thought, *I'm dying*, or *I have AIDS*. She had no one to turn to and was too embarrassed to share her secret with anyone else. It wasn't something that she wanted the world to know. And even though she desperately needed someone to talk to and a shoulder to lean on, it was a secret that she would take to her grave.

Honey peeped her head inside Tasha's room and knocked on the door, snapping Amra out of her thoughts. Amra looked up and saw Honey walk into the room.

"Tasha, can I talk to you for a minute?"

Tasha didn't really feel like talking to Honey. Every time she tried to talk to her about Troy, Honey just added unwanted pressure to the situation. Tasha knew that Honey would say what she needed to say.

"Amra, can we have a minute?" Honey asked.

Amra nodded her head. "I'll be in the living room with Mimi."

After Amra left the room, Honey sat down across from Tasha. "So, what are you doing tonight?"

"Honey, come on now. Cut the bullshit. I know you. You didn't have Amra leave the room so you could ask me what I got up for tonight."

"Okay, you're right. I want to know what you're going to do about Joe. I mean, I know how you feel about him, but you have to help the detective get him."

"I don't know what I'm going to do about him. I know I love him—"

"Love ain't got shit to do with it. Tasha, we are hot right now. This is the only way to resolve it."

Tasha looked Honey in the eye. "Resolve it? It's funny how you keep telling me to fix this. It's real fucked up how it's up to me to make this right. I'm not the only one who was at Keys' house that night." Tasha was furious. Honey was living her regular life, and Amra and Mimi were clueless about the situation, all while she was trying to clean up their mess.

Honey stood up and got in Tasha's face. "You're the one who set Keys up in the first place," she said, pointing her finger in Tasha's face. "We only robbed him so that you and Amra could get the money for Ms. Pat. Then, you fucked up and only gave him one pill. If you would have given him both, he never would have woken up, and Amra never would have killed him. You got us into this bullshit, so you need to get us out. Fuck Joe! That nigga ain't done shit for you. We're the ones who had your back and been there when you needed us, not him." Honey walked out of the room.

Tasha plopped down on her bed in despair. *She's right. I did get us into this.* She picked up her cell phone and dialed Joe's number.

"Hello?"

Tasha wanted to hang up the phone. She didn't want to go through with Troy's plan, but she didn't have a choice. "Hi, it's me," she said sweetly.

"What up? Are you ready?"

"No, I was just calling you to tell you I will be ready at nine." She gave him directions to the house.

"All right, I'll see you then."

Tasha hung up the phone and walked over to her dresser and stared at her reflection in the mirror. *I can do this.*

Honey couldn't believe that Tasha would even think about betraying her. She never thought that Tasha would fuck her over, but she knew how she felt about Joe. *I have to find a way to get out of this shit, just in case she doesn't go through with it.* Honey refused to go to jail for some shit that she didn't do. *I'm not the one who killed Keys.*

Honey thought hard about how she could fix their dilemma. She didn't know if Tasha could go through with it, and didn't want to leave it up to chance. *I need to think of a Plan-B. Amra and Mimi don't even know about it. I still don't think that they need to know. I have to figure this out on my own. The less they know, the better. They will just panic and confuse things even more.*

She regretted helping to rob Keys, but at the time, her friends needed her, which was why she'd agreed to do it. *I wouldn't be caught up in this shit now.*

Tasha looked in the mirror, hoping that the outfit she had chosen looked as good as she thought it did. She rubbed her sweaty hands together and took deep breaths, trying to calm herself. She didn't want Joe to pick up on her vibe. *He should be here any minute.* She closed her eyes. *I can do this.* Her cell phone rang loudly, jolting her already rattled nerves. "Hello?"

"You remember what you have to do, right?"

Tasha grimaced when she heard Troy's deep voice on the other end of the phone. "Yeah, I know."

"Tasha, remember what's at stake. I want a conviction." Troy got off on putting drug dealers behind bars. "I want something that can put him away for a long time. I want you to find out who he's getting it from, when he's getting it, and where it's going down. That's your job, understood?"

Tasha listened to Troy's commands, and instantly began to feel like a traitor. "I understand." She hung up her phone and put it on vibrate. Just as she was about to put the phone in her purse, it vibrated. *What the fuck does he want?* "Hello?"

"I'm outside your crib. You ready?"

The sound of Joe's voice made her smile. "I'm on my way out."

Tasha walked out of her room and bumped into Honey on the way out the door. Both girls stopped and stared each other down before going on their way.

Tasha smiled when she saw Joe waiting at the curb in a black Mercedes Benz. He reached over the seat and opened the door, and when she hopped in, he pulled off. He dropped the top down, and Tasha's hair blew in the wind. They cruised through the city streets, enjoying each other's company. The night was perfect.

Joe reached over and grabbed her hand. "Why are you so quiet?"

Tasha intertwined her fingers in his. "Sorry. I just got a lot on my mind."

"You want to talk about it?"

Tasha shook her head no, and sat back in her seat, trying to relax.

"Where you wanna go? I don't really know much about Flint. You tell me what's up."

"A new club on the North Side just opened not too long ago. We can go there."

Joe nodded his head and punched the gas, causing Tasha's head to jerk back. She started to laugh and threw her hands in the air, letting the wind rush between her fingers.

After they pulled into the parking lot of the club, Joe cut off the car. He hit the hazard lights and then hit the AC button, and a small compartment popped out of the dashboard. He reached into his waistline and put his gun and a couple stacks of money inside.

Tasha laughed. "You got some ol' James Bond type shit going on."

Joe smiled. "Come on."

The club had a mellow vibe when they walked in.

Everyone seemed to be enjoying themselves. They found a table and sat down, and Joe ordered a bottle of Merlot.

"Why did you come to Flint?"

Joe sat back in his chair. "A business venture."

Tasha shook her head and sipped on the wine. She was nervous. She hadn't been around Joe in months, and it felt different. "So, you plan on staying here?"

"Nah. When the money runs out, I'm gone."

Tasha reached across the table and grabbed Joe's hands. "I missed you."

Joe was quiet for a moment. "I missed you too. I thought about you a lot after you left."

Tasha put her head down and instantly felt a streak of guilt. "I thought about you too. It's like I've been counting the days until I can come home."

Joe looked her in the eye. "What's stopping you?"

Tasha froze for a moment, not knowing how to answer his question. In her mind, she was saying, *I have to help set you up.* "Business."

Joe laughed. "Business, huh?"

Tasha smiled. "What? You the only person who got stuff to handle?"

Joe shook his head and didn't reply.

After Tasha stopped thinking about setting Joe up, she relaxed, and they had a good time. They talked and caught up on old times. Everything he did reminded her of why she was so infatuated with him. The way he walked, talked, dressed . . . just everything about him had her hooked. Joe told her about what was happening back home, and she listened closely. She missed the sound of his voice.

They sat in the club for a couple hours, but when it got too crowded. they decided to leave. Joe took Tasha back to his hotel. She walked into the room and sat down on the bed. She smiled to herself as she watched Joe walk over to her. She loved his brown complexion and his strong jawbone.

Out of the blue, Tasha asked, "When I come back home, will you still be waiting for me?"

Joe sat down next to her. "I ain't gon' lie to you. I have been with other women since you left. It doesn't mean shit though. I don't know . . . it's something about you. Them other bitches don't mean shit to me. They can't compare to you."

Tasha's heart dropped when Joe said that he had been with other women, even though she didn't really expect him to wait.

Joe saw the look of disappointment spread across her face. "When you get back, it's me and you."

Tasha smiled and kissed him on his cheek. "I love you, Joe."

Joe lightly wiped away the tear that slid down Tasha's face. He lay down on his back. Tasha lay beside him and put her head against his chest. She could hear his heart beating, and the rhythmic thud soothed her as she snuggled close to his body. He put his arm around her body and held her.

"We should go back home," Tasha whispered.

"I got business here. I can't just up and leave right now, ma." He kissed the top of her head, and Tasha closed her eyes and sighed deeply.

They lay together in silence, enjoying the time they were spending together. Hours passed, and they didn't speak. All they did was hold each other. Tasha held onto Joe as if her life depended on it. It felt good to be near him. It was the first time she felt safe since leaving Flint.

"I love you," she said.

When Joe didn't respond, Tasha sat up and looked at him. He was knocked out and looked too peaceful to wake. She kissed him softly on the lips, and then got up and took a cab back to Tammy's house.

Chapter Nineteen

The sound of the alarm beeped loudly, and Joe hit the snooze button. He looked over at the clock. It said 10:00 A.M. He stood up slowly and wiped the sleep out of his eyes. He sat back down as if in a daze. He thought about going back to sleep, but the vibrations of his phone made him think otherwise. He picked it up off the nightstand and looked at the number. He shook his head and said in a groggy voice, "Another day, another dollar."

Joe walked into the hotel's bathroom wearing nothing but his Calvin Klein boxers. He looked in the mirror and splashed warm water on his face. He put his hands on the side of the sink and leaned forward, holding his head down. *Today is my last day on the grind. I can't do this shit no more. I'm taking my money and getting out of the game. I made a quarter-mil before I turned twentyfive. Fuck that! I've seen greed send niggas straight to the pen. I'm out!* As he brushed his teeth, he thought about the exchange he had to make later that day. He was going to make this the last transaction and return to New York.

Joe got fully dressed and put on his leather coat. He reached in the pocket and pulled out a Tiffany's jewelry box. He opened it up, and the 18-karat diamond ring glistened in the sunlight streaming through the window. *I'm gonna ask Tasha tonight.* He had never met a woman as beautiful and intelligent as Tasha. He loved her, and wasn't going to let her slip out of his grasp.

"I overheard him talking to someone on the phone last night. He is supposed to make a drop-off tonight at . . ." Tasha felt a tear stream down her cheek, and her heart began to pound harder and harder. *I can't do this. I should just warn Joe, or make him leave home with me. We could leave tonight.* Tasha was looking for an escape, a way to leave the madness behind and get away with Joe. She took the phone away from her ear, her lips quivering uncontrollably as she realized she was about to snitch on Joe, the only man she ever loved.

Troy yelled through the phone, "Hello? Hello?"

Tasha put the phone back to her ear. "I'm here."

"Where, Tasha? Finish telling me where."

She took a deep breath. "Tonight at eleven o'clock, he is supposed to . . ." She stopped. *I can't!*

Troy quickly grew frustrated, "Tell me! Tonight at eleven . . . where, Tasha? Say it!"

Tasha couldn't speak. The only thing she could think about was how kind and gentle Joe was to her, how much he loved her, and how well he always treated her. It tore her up inside that she was being forced to do this.

"He is supposed to be dropping off a couple kilos to a dude named Benny at the old steel factory down by the river."

A big smile spread across Troy's face. "That's a good girl!"

Tasha hung up the phone and slumped onto the floor crying. She slammed her hands against her face, regretting that she'd let the words out of her mouth. She whispered, "I'm sorry. Baby, I'm so sorry!"

Honey stood in Tasha's doorway watching her cry to herself. She had overheard her whole conversation. "Fuck that nigga, Tasha!"

Tasha wiped her eyes and looked back at Honey with a confused expression.

"That nigga would not go to jail for you, Tasha. You need to get your shit together."

Tasha got up off the floor and softly said, "Bitch, get out of my room!"

Honey put her hands on her hips. "Bitch, this is my auntie's house. I ain't got to go nowhere."

Tasha rolled her eyes and stormed out of the room, bumping past Honey. "I don't have time for this shit." *I'm getting the fuck out of here. After this shit is over, I'm on the first flight back to New York.* She picked up her cell phone and dialed Amra's number.

Amra sat in the doctor's office when her phone rang. The caller ID displayed Tasha's name. "Hello?" "Amra, we're leaving. This ain't for us. I'm trying to be out of town by tomorrow night."

"I know. I been thinking the same thing. I'm ready to go back home. I need to be home with my momma right now."

"I'm going to get the tickets now."

Amra saw the nurse motion for her. "Tasha, I love you. You are my sister, and I love you more than anything. Always remember that."

Tasha had to laugh. "Damn, girl! You act like we ain't gon' see each other no more. Quit tripping. Anyway, we are leaving ASAP, so when you get back to Tammy's, pack your stuff."

"I love you."

"I love you too."

Tasha stood outside Tammy's house and called a cab. She wanted to get to the airport and buy their tickets. Honey and Tasha didn't see eye to eye on the Troy situation, and Tasha was getting real tired of Honey and her attitudes. She sat on the curb waiting for the taxi to come. Feeling so alone and so afraid, she couldn't help but cry. She didn't know what was going to happen to Joe.

The next thing she knew, a car pulled up in front of her. "Get in," she heard someone say.

Tasha popped her head up and was startled to see Joe. She quickly wiped her face and got into his car.

He kissed her softly on the lips. "Are you all right?"

Tasha shook her head. "No, and I don't want to talk about it."

Even though Joe wanted to know what was bothering her, he just held her hand with his right hand and pulled off, his left hand on the steering wheel. "Tonight I have something planned for us."

Tasha tried one last time to convince him to leave. "Let's just leave, Joe, me and you. Let's go back home right now."

Joe rubbed his smooth face. "I feel you. I'm ready to leave too, but not tonight. I have to handle one last thing. Tomorrow we can be on the first flight out of here."

Tasha realized she couldn't stop Joe from making that transaction she had tipped Troy off about. Joe reached over and held her hand while he drove, and his touch made tears form in her eyes. She closed her eyes, trying to make them go away. *I'm sorry, baby! I'm so sorry!*

Joe looked over at her. "I love you, Tasha."

His words only broke her heart even more. She opened her eyes and looked him dead in his. "I love you too." Tasha held on tight to his hand as she watched the street signs pass her by.

Joe pulled up to a hotel and parked the car. Tasha followed him to his room and reluctantly walked inside. She looked at the clock that sat beside the bed and knew it wouldn't be long before Troy put him in handcuffs.

"Baby, let's go. Let's go far away from here, just me and you."

"Tasha, that sounds good, but I have to handle this one thing. I told you, we're on the first flight out tomorrow." Joe walked over to the closet and grabbed a briefcase. "Now, I want you to wait here for me, and when I get back, we celebrate." Joe kissed her softly on the cheek before walking out the door.

Tasha wanted to say something so badly. Everything inside of her wanted to stop him from walking out that door. Her heart told her to stop him, but her mind was thinking of her freedom and the freedom of all her friends. She dropped her chin to her chest and felt her heart beat fast.

It felt like a baboon was on the inside of her, fighting to get out.

Just as Joe was about to close the door, she called out to him, "Joe!" Don't go!" The words echoed in her head, but, "I love you!" slipped out of her mouth.

Joe smirked. "Tasha, I love you too. After this, it's over. Our life together will begin soon."

His words made what she was going through all the more difficult to bear. As soon as he closed the door, she dropped to her knees and cried uncontrollably, realizing there was nothing left to do. She balled up her fists and beat the floor, trying to take her anger out on something. Her heart was filled with guilt; she loved Joe, and he loved her. She yearned to be with him, to take back everything she'd done wrong in her life and be with him. She stared around the room hopelessly. She lay down on the floor and balled up into a fetal position.

She felt her cell phone vibrate on her hip, and quickly reached for it. She looked at the caller ID and saw Troy's name flashing across the screen. The sight of his name enraged her, and she began to tear up the room. She threw the lamp against the wall, breaking it into pieces. "Aghh-hhh!" she screamed. "I hate you!" She tipped the TV off the stand onto the floor.

Panting, she stood in the middle of the hotel room, trying to catch her breath. Tears flowed down her face as she realized that she had made the biggest mistake of her life. *"Joe!"* she screamed at the top of her lungs. Tasha raced out the room at full speed, heading toward the spot she had tipped Troy off about.

Joe drove his car ten blocks up from the hotel he had just left. It was dark outside, and only the moonlight illuminated the abandoned warehouse. He parked his Mercedes in the back, turned off his cell phone, grabbed the briefcase, and cocked his gun before putting it in his waistline. *One more time . . . one more time, and I'm finished. I can't wait to get back to Tasha and ask her to be my wife.*

Joe exited his car and slowly walked to the back entrance. He opened the door and noticed that he was the first to arrive. He looked at his watch and cursed softly to himself. "Damn! Where he at?"

Tasha was running full speed, sprinting down the street. She only had a few minutes to reach her destination. She dialed Joe's number as she ran, but got no answer. *I have to stop him from making the drop-off.*

The ten blocks from the hotel to the warehouse seemed more like a million. Tasha felt her legs tightening with each stride, and a cramp forming in her stomach. She thought she would pass out, but she didn't stop. Her lungs were on fire, and as fast as she tried to run, it seemed to be taking her forever.

Troy was waiting around the block from the warehouse in a gray unmarked van with surveillance monitors and tape recorders. He had set up hidden cameras and bugs to view and hear all that was happening inside the warehouse, and the only thing he had to do was wait. He also had a ground team waiting to rush in and arrest Joe.

He had a big smile on his face, knowing he had a conviction sitting in the palm of his hand. He grabbed his walkie-talkie and said to his team, "Don't make any moves until the transaction is made. We need to catch him red-handed."

Mimi sat in her living room, high as a kite and without a care in the world. She was smoking a fat blunt and rolling another one that she was gonna fire up as soon as she finished the one she was on. She wondered where everybody else was. Her love for weed had grown, but she was low on cash, and her supply would be running out soon. She picked up her cell phone and called Manolo.

"Hello?"

Mimi hadn't spoken to him in months. "Hey, Manolo," she said sweetly.

Manolo recognized her voice but didn't reply.

"Manolo, you got a job for me? I need some cash."

Manolo laughed quietly. "Yeah, baby, I got a job for you. I'm on some new shit now though. I got this escort service I'm starting. You wit' it?"

Mimi frowned. "Escort? You pimping now?"

"I'm making money. I'm expanding and taking the Manolo Mamis to another level. You called me. If you ain't with it—"

Desperate for money and attention, Mimi quickly interjected, "Nah, Nolo. You know I'm with it."

Mimi had no idea what she was getting herself into. She had just officially become Manolo's first ho in what would be a very profitable prostitution ring.

Honey threw the clothes into her bag. "Stupid-ass bitch!" she mumbled to herself, referring to Tasha. "I'm not going down for this shit." She was already anticipating that Tasha wouldn't go through with the plan. She grabbed the money that she kept under her bed and packed that into the bag too. She hadn't heard from Tasha all day, and didn't know if she had gone through with it or not. She wasn't waiting around to find out though.

Honey stuffed the rest of her clothes into the black gym bag and sat down on her bed. *I am not taking the fall for Keys' murder. Fuck that! I'm gonna get out of this, no matter what. I don't give a damn about nobody but me.* She took the money from the shoebox that she and Tasha had stored their savings in, close to fifty thousand which was supposed to be for a salon, and stuffed it in her Louis Vuitton purse, not caring that half of it belonged to Tasha.

Tasha's desperation was growing as she ran down the brightly-lit streets of Flint. She was running so fast that the soles of her feet hurt as they hit the concrete, and her heart felt like it was going to burst. She saw the warehouse a block ahead. All she had to do was make it there.

When she reached the fence that surrounded the building, she looked around cautiously, praying that Troy Smith had not beaten her there. She didn't see him, or anybody else for that matter, so she crawled through the hole in the fence. She saw Joe's car near the back of the building and ran past it, trying to find an entrance to the building.

Tasha found the front door, opened it, and slowly walked inside the dimly-lit warehouse. She wanted to turn back around, but it was too late now. She had come too far. *I have to find him*. She yelled, "Joe!" as she made her way to the back of the warehouse. She walked around the corner and saw the silhouette of two people. "Joe! Joe! No, it's a setup!"

Joe said almost in a whisper, "Tasha?"

The man that Joe was doing business with put his hand on his gun and frowned. "What the fuck is going on?" He stepped back slowly.

Joe put his hands up. "Hold up, hold up." He turned to Tasha and asked, "What the hell are you doing?"

Tasha ran over to him, still out of breath from her ten-block run. "It's a setup. The police are on their way."

Joe looked at Tasha in confusion, and in the midst of the chaos, the man announced, "I'm out of here."

Tasha began to cry hysterically. "I'm sorry, baby. I'm so sorry. I never wanted you to go to jail."

"What do you mean, you don't want me to go to jail? What are you talking about?" Joe grabbed her by the shoulders, trying to get her to stop crying and tell him what was going on.

Tasha looked up at Joe and said, "I told him. I told the detective about the drop-off. I-I didn't want to. Baby, he made me. He was blackmailing me!"

Joe wasn't sure he had heard her correctly. "What?"

Before she could respond, he heard the police sirens. He dropped his bag and stared Tasha in the eyes in total disappointment. He couldn't believe what he'd just heard. His eyes watered, but he didn't let one tear fall. "Why? Why the fuck would you do this? I love you. It was me and you against the world."

Tasha could see the pain in his face, but before she could explain herself, the lights from the police cars flashed as the police approached.

Joe began to back away from Tasha.

She reached out her hand to him and screamed through sweat and tears, "Please don't leave me! Joe, please! I'm sorry! I love you!"

Joe was filled with pain. He loved her more than he loved himself, but she was dirty. She had set him up, and that wasn't something he was willing to forgive.

The more steps he took toward the back door, the more her heart, stomach, and mind ached. She could feel her heart beat in her throat, and her stomach felt as if it had a bowling ball sitting in it.

Joe wanted desperately to grab her hand and take her with him. A part of him loved her more than anything, was willing to forgive and forget, and still wanted to take her in his arms and make her his wife. But another part of him, the part that had been raised by the law of the streets, wanted to smack the shit out of her for her deep betrayal, if not kill her. Her disloyalty had cost them both the love they shared. That part of Joe would not allow him to love Tasha. If he did keep her around, he would just treat her like a 'hood rat, and he knew deep in his heart that she deserved better than that. Joe thought about all these things in a split second. He looked at Tasha one last time, and then took off through the back entrance.

She stood in the middle of the warehouse, helpless and in despair as the police rushed in, their guns drawn. "Freeze!" they yelled at her. "Where is he?"

Tasha pointed to the staircase at the front of the room. "He went up to the roof." She knew that would give Joe enough time to flee the scene.

As the swarm of officers ran up the stairs in pursuit of Joe, Tasha ran toward the front door. Just as she stepped out, Troy Smith was waiting for her.

Troy knew she had sent his officers on a wild goose chase. "Where is he?"

"I don't know."

Troy grabbed her arm. "Where is he?" he yelled.

When Tasha didn't reply, he turned her around and applied his handcuffs to her small wrists. "Bitch, I hope he was worth it. You have the right to remain silent. Anything you say can and will be used against you in the court of law . . ."

Tasha sat in the police precinct waiting to be fingerprinted, and her emotions were running wild. She was hurt and lonely, but most of all, she was scared. Getting arrested was freaking her out.

After a two-hour interrogation, Tasha was sure the police did not have anything on her. *They can't pin this on me. There were no fingerprints left at Keys' house. It's my word against his. Those pictures don't prove anything. They won't hold up in court. For all they know, Keys was alive when I left. For all the shit we went through, I would never rat on any of my girls.*

Troy walked out of the interrogation room with a big smile on his face. Tasha even smiled back, knowing he didn't have enough evidence against her or any of her girls. He walked over to Tasha and bent over to whisper in her ear, "I got you!"

Tasha looked him dead in his eyes and remained silent.

Troy told one of the policemen sitting at a desk, "Issue an arrest warrant for Amra Rodgers—accessory to first-degree murder!"

Tasha's eyes shot open, and she jerked her head up at the sound of her best friend's name. Her heart began to pound, and a lump formed in her throat. *How did he find out about Amra?*

Troy had a cocky look on his face. He laughed. "I see you don't have all that lip now." He told one of his fellow officers, "Tell the witness in the Keys murder case she's free to go."

The officer nodded his head and walked over to the interrogation room. He opened the door, and Tasha couldn't believe what she saw. Honey walked out of the interrogation room, shook Troy's hand, and was walking out of the police station with a smirk on her face.

Tasha whispered to herself, "What da . . ." Honey had snitched on her. The tears started to form in her eyes, and a single tear fell as she lowered her head and prepared herself for the inevitable, regretting the day she'd stepped foot in the murder capital, Flint, Michigan.

Epilogue

I told you that you wouldn't be disappointed in my story. It's kind of fucked up how it all ended between us, ain't it? We were the original Manolo Mamis, the baddest bitches in the game, taking niggas for everything they got. We were living the fast life until things started to catch up to us. Through this experience, I have learned that everything you do in life has a consequence. For every one of your actions, the world has a reaction just waiting for you. I had to learn this the hard way.

An eight-year sentence in a state prison is hard to adjust to, but hey, that's karma for you. I knew robbing Keys was wrong, but I did it anyway. It wasn't for greed though. I can honestly say that. I was just in a bind and needed some fast cash, and Keys was the only man in town who had the type of money that I needed.

Ms. Pat was depending on Amra, and Amra was depending on me. I never thought anybody would get hurt. I definitely didn't think that anyone would die. That one night was when my life started to spiral out of control and gave Detective Troy Smith what he needed to blackmail me. It's what made me set up Joe . . . Jamaica Joe.

When I think about him, my heart aches. I loved him so much, but more importantly, he loved me, and I almost got him arrested. I've written him many letters, but they always go unanswered. I do still love him though, with all my heart. I do. I just wish he could understand that I didn't have a choice. By the time I realized I'd made a mistake, it was too late. I tried to fix it, I really did, and I'm doing time to prove it. I didn't snitch because I'm a real bitch, point-blank. I could have let Troy arrest him, but instead, I took the fall. Now my pretty ass is in prison.

It's crazy how things turn out. I guess I had two consequences: One, I'm rotting in this cage; and, two, I lost the one person who I could depend on. Some of you might say that I deserve what I got, that I had it coming to me. I don't know. I just know that if I could go back, I would do things a lot differently. We all would.

Amra was my girl. When I think about her, it always brings tears to my eyes. She was my best friend and the most beautiful person who has ever graced this earth. She was hardheaded though, and made a lot of bad choices, which may have cost her her life. I remember telling her time and time again to slow down. I tried to tell her that there were other ways to get money, and that she didn't always have to tempt a man with sex. She didn't listen though, and sometimes I wish I'd paid more attention to her. Maybe I could have stopped her before she started getting out of control.

One thing I can say about Amra though, is that she loved life. She rode that mu'fucka until the wheels fell off. Her wheels just fell off a little earlier than most. She had sex with more men than even she could keep track of. Amra contracted HIV, and caught it so late that it progressed quickly. She died of AIDS at the tender age of twenty. God rest her soul, she died a couple of months after my arrest. I didn't even know she had it.

I guess I always saw the signs—the sore throats, the fatigue, the sores on her legs. Maybe I just didn't want to face the reality that my best friend— no, my *sister*—was dying. Her death hit me hard. It was like my world had filled with water, and I was struggling to find air, to take one deep breath.

Mimi was my girl too. A hustler at heart, she was the originator of our lovely phrase, "Fuck me, Pay me!" I have to admit, at first I was a little bit skeptical about befriending her. It seemed like she was shady, but she was actually the exact opposite. She was just a real chick. Mimi never really did much. When I first met her, she had a dream of owning her own salon, but it seemed like the more I got to know her, I realized that her dream was just that . . . a dream. She never really had a hustle plan to get herself out of the 'hood. It's where she felt most comfortable, where she belonged.

Mimi was a 'hood rat. I've seen her count out thousands of dollars, but today she is working for Manolo. Even though she ain't doing nothing but tricking, the bitch stays paid. Manolo has to watch her back though, because with all the niggas we robbed, she has made a lot of enemies. And even though she stays on her grind, it doesn't lead her anywhere. Mimi's lack of ambition would forever keep her in the 'hood.

I've talked to Manolo a couple of times since my arrest. He keeps my commissary straight and says he's got a job for me when I get out. I think he wants me to run the Manolo Mamis. I just might take him up on his offer.

It seems like Honey could have helped Mimi out. I mean, that's her cousin and all. Word on the streets is that Honey is sitting on bread. After that bitch testified against me, rumor has it that she came across a lot of money. Grimy-ass bitch!

Honey was the one who introduced us to the game, always the one with fly clothes and jewelry, and we listened to her when she bragged about how she had gotten some dude to buy it for her.

Life can be so unfair sometimes, especially from where I'm sitting. Honey never really received a consequence for all of the dirt she's done. It seems like she got off easy. I don't know. Maybe everything hasn't caught up to her yet. She was once like a big sister to me. It seemed like she was always looking out for me, always protecting me. I thought that we had mad love for each other, but she is like so many other bitches in the 'hood; you never know what hidden agendas they have up their sleeves.

So she's living good now, but hold up! You haven't heard the most fucked-up part about it. The bitch is fucking with Joe now! I heard she got his name tattooed on her back and everything. Supposedly she's pregnant by him. I guess she found her meal ticket. Dirty bitch! I always knew she was a little bit too interested in my nigga.

Please believe me, you reap what you sow. She just hasn't gotten what's coming to her yet. Karma is real, and eventually everybody will have to face it. I know what's coming to Honey though.

The bitch is hiding out in Detroit, while Jamaica Joe handles his business in Flint. I still can't believe she ended up with my man, but I guess I'll see her when I see her.

I go in front of the parole board next week, and my lawyer is sure that I'll be released early for good behavior. I've been in here for four years. I think I've served my time.

I can't wait to get out in these streets. I'm gon' make this money by helping Manolo groom a new generation of Manolo Mamis. According to Mimi, those bitches think they the shit, but they need to learn the game, and I'm just the one to teach it to them.

I tell you what, though. There will never be a group of bitches like us—Tasha, Amra, Mimi, and even that bitch, Honey. We had the game on smash.

Anyway, that's my story, so until next time . . . *One!*